GW01398596

The Heist

Thrillers, Volume 4

William James Brown

Published by Serene Sky Publishing, 2024.

THE HEIST

First edition. November 24, 2024.

ISBN: 979-8227275295

Written by William James Brown.

Table of Contents

To those who dare to dream big, who defy the odds and push the boundaries of what's possible. To the risk-takers, the rebels, and the ones who never give up—even when the world says they should. This one's for you.

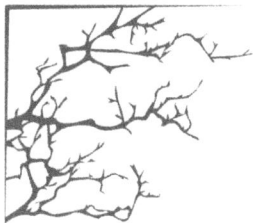

Chapter 1: The Plan

Lucas "Lucky" Kane leaned back in his leather chair, the dim light casting shadows across his chiseled features. He stared at the map of Fort Knox spread out on the mahogany table before him, his mind racing through every detail of the heist. The room was silent, save for the occasional crackle of the fireplace. Tonight was the night he would unveil his grand plan, and he needed every detail to be perfect.

He glanced at his watch, noting that his team would be arriving soon. Lucas was a man in his late thirties, with sharp blue eyes and a confident demeanor. His nickname, "Lucky," wasn't just a moniker; it was a testament to his incredible ability to turn the odds in his favor, no matter how stacked they were against him. He had pulled off some of the most daring heists in the country, but this one—this one would be the crown jewel of his career.

The first to arrive was Emma Hayes, the tech genius. At twenty-eight, Emma was a prodigy, with a mind sharper than any computer she hacked. She had auburn hair tied back in a ponytail and wore glasses that gave her a deceptively innocent look. But behind those glasses was a brain capable of breaking into the most secure systems in the world.

"Hey, Lucas," Emma said as she entered, setting her laptop on the table. "Hope I'm not too early."

"Right on time, Emma," Lucas replied, offering a rare smile. "You know I like punctuality."

Next came Jack "Smooth" Taylor, the con artist. Jack was in his mid-thirties, with a charming smile and an aura of charisma that could win over even the most skeptical hearts. He wore a tailored suit, looking every bit the gentleman thief. Jack had a knack for slipping into any role, a talent that had saved the team more than once.

"Lucas, Emma," Jack greeted, taking a seat and smoothing his suit. "This better be good. I had to ditch a rather promising poker game for this."

Lucas smirked. "Trust me, Jack, this will be worth your while."

Finally, Carl "Tank" Johnson entered the room. At six-foot-five and built like a linebacker, Carl was the muscle of the team. He had a no-nonsense attitude and was fiercely loyal to Lucas. His bald head and intense gaze made him an imposing figure, but to those who knew him, he was a gentle giant—unless you crossed him.

"Boss," Carl nodded at Lucas, then grunted a greeting to Emma and Jack before taking a seat.

With the team assembled, Lucas stood and walked to the head of the table. He pressed a button on a remote, and the projector hummed to life, displaying detailed schematics of Fort Knox on the screen.

"Thank you all for coming," Lucas began, his voice steady and authoritative. "What I'm about to propose is the most ambitious plan we've ever undertaken. The target: Fort Knox."

A collective gasp filled the room. Even Emma, who was usually unflappable, looked stunned.

"Fort Knox?" Jack echoed, his eyes wide. "You're serious?"

"Dead serious," Lucas confirmed. "We've pulled off some incredible jobs in the past, but this... this is the ultimate prize. The gold reserves of Fort Knox. If we succeed, we'll be set for life."

Carl leaned forward, his brow furrowing. "What's the plan, boss? This place is a fortress."

Lucas nodded. "It is, but every fortress has its weaknesses. Emma, if you would?"

Emma stood and took over, her fingers flying over the keyboard of her laptop. The screen changed to show various security systems, blueprints, and guard schedules.

"Fort Knox has multiple layers of security," Emma explained. "The outer perimeter is guarded by heavily armed military personnel. Inside, there are motion detectors, infrared sensors, biometric locks, and the vault itself, which is surrounded by solid granite walls and a sophisticated alarm system."

She paused, letting the enormity of the task sink in. "However, we've identified a few vulnerabilities. First, there's a scheduled power maintenance on the third Thursday of every month. During this time, the security systems switch to backup generators, which have a five-second delay. It's a small window, but it's a start."

Jack whistled low. "Five seconds isn't much."

"It's enough," Lucas interjected. "With precise timing and coordination, we can exploit that window to gain initial access."

Emma continued, "Additionally, I've managed to acquire the layout of the security room. If we can take control of that room, we can disable the alarms and cameras for a short period. This will be Carl's job."

Carl nodded, his expression resolute. "Leave it to me."

"The biggest challenge," Emma went on, "is the biometric lock on the vault. It requires both a retinal scan and fingerprint authorization from the commanding officer on duty."

Lucas stepped in. "That's where Jack comes in. Jack, you'll need to get close to the officer, gain his trust, and obtain his biometric data."

Jack raised an eyebrow. "And how exactly do I do that?"

Lucas smiled. "Leave that to your charm and improvisation skills. We'll provide you with the tools you need, but the rest is up to you."

Jack sighed, running a hand through his hair. "No pressure, then."

"Once we're inside," Lucas continued, "we'll have a limited amount of time to get the gold and get out before the backup systems kick in and the alarms sound. Timing is everything."

He looked around the table, meeting each team member's eyes. "This job is risky—more so than anything we've ever done. But the rewards are beyond anything we've ever imagined. Are you all in?"

Emma was the first to respond, her determination evident. "I'm in. We can do this."

Jack followed, his grin returning. "Count me in. I've always wanted to pull off the impossible."

Carl pounded his fist on the table. "You know I've got your back, boss. Let's do this."

Lucas nodded, feeling a surge of pride for his team. "Good. Now let's go over the plan in detail."

The next few hours were spent discussing every aspect of the heist, from the infiltration to the escape. Lucas outlined each step meticulously, ensuring that everyone knew their role and the timing involved. They debated the risks and devised contingency plans for various scenarios.

As the night wore on, the initial tension began to ease, replaced by a sense of camaraderie and shared purpose. The team members, each bringing their unique skills to the table, started to see the plan come together.

By the time they wrapped up, the fire had burned down to embers, and exhaustion was beginning to show on their faces. But there was also a glint of excitement in their eyes, a spark of anticipation for the challenge ahead.

"Get some rest," Lucas said, standing and stretching. "We've got a lot of work to do in the coming weeks. And remember, discretion is key. No one outside this room can know about our plans."

The team nodded in agreement, gathering their belongings and heading out into the night. Lucas watched them go, a sense of satisfaction settling over him. They had a long road ahead, but with this team and this plan, he believed they could pull off the heist of the century.

As the door closed behind the last of his crew, Lucas returned to the table, staring at the map of Fort Knox. He traced his finger along the route they would take, his mind already running through the plan again, searching for any overlooked details.

This heist would be the pinnacle of his career, the ultimate challenge. And he was ready for it.

THE FOLLOWING MORNING, Lucas called a private meeting with Emma to discuss the technological aspects in greater detail. They met in a small, nondescript office in downtown Los Angeles, far from prying eyes. Emma had brought a portable server and several laptops to simulate the security systems they would encounter.

"Alright, Lucas," Emma began, powering up her equipment. "We need to talk about the specifics of breaching their network. It's going to be tricky, even with the power maintenance window."

Lucas nodded, his focus intense. "Walk me through it."

Emma pulled up a schematic on her screen. "Fort Knox uses a multi-layered security system, as I mentioned. During the maintenance, the primary systems will switch to backup, which gives us that five-second delay. But there's more to it than just a simple switch-over."

She highlighted sections of the schematic. "The backup generators are linked to an independent network that runs parallel to the main system. To disable the alarms and cameras, we need to simultaneously hack both networks. I'll need to create a custom virus that can infiltrate both without being detected."

Lucas frowned. "How long will that take?"

Emma sighed, tapping her keyboard thoughtfully. "Creating the virus isn't the hard part. The challenge is making it undetectable and ensuring it activates at the exact moment we need it to. I'll need at least two weeks to develop and test it."

"Do it," Lucas said. "What about the biometric lock?"

Emma pulled up another schematic. "The biometric lock is a dual-authentication system, requiring both a retinal scan and a fingerprint. I can create a device to capture and replicate these, but Jack will need to get close enough to the commanding officer to use it."

Lucas rubbed his chin. "Jack's good, but this is pushing even his limits. What can we do to increase his chances?"

"I can design a distraction to give him more time," Emma suggested. "Maybe a temporary malfunction in the security system that requires the officer's attention."

"Good idea," Lucas agreed

. "Do it. And let's work on a backup plan in case something goes wrong. We can't afford any slip-ups."

Over the next few days, the team worked tirelessly on their respective tasks. Emma locked herself in her workshop, surrounded by screens and servers, her fingers flying over the keyboard as she coded the virus. Jack began his preparations, studying the commanding officer's routines and habits, figuring out how best to approach him. Carl trained rigorously, ensuring he was in peak physical condition for the heist.

Lucas coordinated everything, keeping the team on track and addressing any issues that arose. He spent hours reviewing the plan, running through simulations, and thinking of every possible scenario that could go wrong.

One evening, as the team gathered for another briefing, Lucas sensed a shift in their dynamic. The initial excitement had given way to a steely determination. They were no longer just talking about the heist; they were living it, breathing it, preparing for every eventuality.

"How's the virus coming along?" Lucas asked Emma as they sat around the table.

"It's almost ready," Emma replied, looking tired but satisfied. "I've run several tests, and it's working as expected. I just need a bit more time to ensure it's foolproof."

"Good," Lucas said. "Jack, how are you doing with the commanding officer?"

Jack grinned, his usual confidence back. "I've got a plan. The officer has a weakness for poker, and there's a high-stakes game coming up. I'll make sure I'm there and win his trust."

"Perfect," Lucas said. "Carl, how's the physical training?"

Carl flexed his massive arms. "I'm ready, boss. Just give me the go-ahead."

Lucas nodded, feeling a swell of pride for his team. They were ready. "Alright, everyone. We've got one week until the heist. Let's make sure everything is in place."

The final week passed in a blur of activity. The team practiced their roles relentlessly, fine-tuning every detail of the plan. They conducted dry runs, timing each step to perfection. Lucas pushed them hard, knowing that their success depended on absolute precision.

On the night before the heist, Lucas called a final meeting. The atmosphere was tense, the weight of what they were about to do hanging heavy in the air.

"This is it," Lucas said, looking each of his team members in the eye. "Tomorrow, we make history. We've planned for every possible scenario, but remember, things can still go wrong. Stay focused, trust each other, and we'll come out of this richer than we ever dreamed."

Emma nodded, her determination evident. "We've got this."

Jack smirked, his confidence unshaken. "I was born for this."

Carl simply grunted, his expression resolute.

"Get some rest," Lucas said. "Tomorrow, we pull off the heist of the century."

As the team dispersed, Lucas lingered in the meeting room, staring at the map of Fort Knox one last time. He knew the risks, but he also knew they were ready. This heist would be his legacy, and he was determined to see it through.

The next day dawned bright and clear, a stark contrast to the tension that gripped the team. They met at a secure location, double-checking their equipment and running through the plan one final time.

Lucas took a deep breath, feeling the adrenaline coursing through his veins. "Alright, team. Let's do this."

As they headed out to execute their plan, Lucas felt a surge of confidence. They were ready. They were prepared. And they were about to pull off the greatest heist in history.

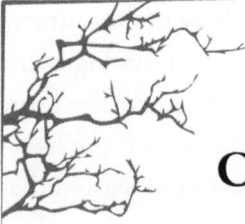

Chapter 2: Recruitment

Flashback to Lucas's Background and Motivations

Lucas "Lucky" Kane's journey to becoming one of the most notorious masterminds in the world of crime was anything but ordinary. Born into a working-class family in a rundown neighborhood of Detroit, Lucas learned the harsh realities of life early on. His father, a factory worker, and his mother, a nurse, worked tirelessly to provide for him and his two younger siblings. Despite their efforts, money was always tight, and Lucas often found himself going to bed hungry.

As a teenager, Lucas was determined to escape the cycle of poverty that trapped his family. He was exceptionally bright and had a knack for numbers and strategy. These skills earned him a scholarship to a prestigious private school, where he was introduced to a world far removed from his own. Here, he saw firsthand the vast chasm between the wealthy elite and the struggling masses.

It was at this school that Lucas's life took a pivotal turn. He became friends with a boy named Jason, whose father was a successful businessman. Through Jason, Lucas got a glimpse of the allure and power that money could buy. However, he also saw the corruption and greed that often accompanied wealth. The disparity between his modest upbringing and the opulence of his new acquaintances fueled a burning desire within him—not just for wealth, but for control and retribution.

Lucas excelled academically, but it was in the game of chess where he truly shined. His strategic mind and ability to anticipate his opponent's moves made him a champion. Chess became a metaphor for his life; every decision was a move on the board, and every move had consequences.

Despite his promising future, Lucas's life was shattered when his father lost his job due to a factory closure. The financial strain led to his parents' separation, and his mother fell ill under the stress. The scholarship he had worked so hard for was in jeopardy as his focus shifted to supporting his family. Desperation drove him to make his first foray into the world of crime—a heist at a local jewelry store, planned meticulously and executed flawlessly. The success of this heist earned him the nickname "Lucky," and more importantly, it provided the funds needed to keep his family afloat.

But one taste of the high-stakes life of crime was enough to hook Lucas. He realized that with his intellect and strategic mind, he could outsmart the system that had failed his family. He vowed to rise above the constraints of his upbringing, and soon, his heists grew in scale and sophistication. Each successful job was a move on the chessboard, bringing him closer to his ultimate goal: a heist so grand that it would secure his legacy forever.

The Recruitment Process for Each Team Member

YEARS OF HONING HIS craft led Lucas to plan the heist of a lifetime—robbing Fort Knox. But to pull off such an audacious plan, he needed a team of specialists, each a master in their field. Lucas set out to recruit the best, starting with Emma Hayes.

Emma Hayes: The Tech Genius

EMMA WAS A LEGEND IN the hacking community. With a background in computer science and engineering, she had once worked for a top cybersecurity firm. Her career took a drastic turn when she discovered her employer was colluding with government agencies to conduct illegal surveillance. Unable to stand the corruption, she exposed the scandal and went underground, using her skills to hack into corrupt corporations and redistribute their wealth.

Lucas tracked Emma down through the dark web, where her reputation as a hacker was unmatched. He knew she would be cautious, so he left a digital trail for her to follow, leading to a secure chat room.

"Who are you?" her message read, the skepticism evident even in text form.

"Someone who appreciates your work," Lucas replied. "I have a proposition that could change your life."

A pause, then: "I'm listening."

Lucas laid out the basics of his plan, careful not to reveal too much. He described the potential rewards and how her skills were crucial to its success. He could almost hear her curiosity piquing.

"Why should I trust you?" she asked.

"Because I'm offering you a chance to take down the very system you despise. And I can assure you, I'm the best at what I do."

After a long silence, Emma responded. "Where do we meet?"

Lucas knew he had her.

Jack "Smooth" Taylor: The Con Artist

NEXT ON LUCAS'S LIST was Jack "Smooth" Taylor, a master of deception and manipulation. Jack had grown up in the foster care system, learning early on how to charm and con his way through life. His natural charisma and quick wit made him a successful con artist, swindling the rich and corrupt out of their fortunes.

Lucas found Jack in Las Vegas, running a high-stakes poker game. Disguised as a wealthy businessman, Lucas joined the game, observing Jack's flawless execution of his cons. After the game, Lucas approached him.

"You're quite the player," Lucas remarked, handing Jack a drink.

Jack eyed him suspiciously. "I don't recall seeing you around here."

"That's because I'm not from around here. I've been looking for someone with your talents."

Jack smirked. "And what talents might those be?"

"The kind that can charm a snake out of its skin. I have a job that requires your unique skills."

Intrigued, Jack listened as Lucas outlined his plan. The allure of a grand heist and the challenge it presented was too tempting for Jack to resist.

"You've got my attention," Jack said. "What's the catch?"

"No catch," Lucas replied. "Just a lot of money and the thrill of a lifetime."

Jack grinned. "Count me in."

Carl "Tank" Johnson: The Muscle

THE FINAL PIECE OF Lucas's puzzle was Carl "Tank" Johnson, a former Marine and a man of immense strength and loyalty. Carl had left the military under less-than-honorable circumstances after a mission went south due to poor leadership. Disillusioned with the system, he found himself working as a bouncer in a seedy bar, using his skills to keep the peace.

Lucas approached Carl at the bar, watching as he effortlessly handled a group of rowdy patrons. After the scuffle, Lucas followed Carl outside.

"Impressive work in there," Lucas said.

Carl turned, his eyes narrowing. "Who the hell are you?"

"Someone who needs your expertise. I have a job that could use a man of your talents."

Carl crossed his arms, skeptical. "And why should I be interested?"

"Because it's a chance to make a lot of money and stick it to a system that's done nothing but screw you over."

Carl studied Lucas for a moment, then nodded. "Alright, I'm listening."

As Lucas explained the plan, Carl's interest grew. The idea of using his skills for a purpose greater than bouncing drunks out of a bar appealed to him.

"Alright," Carl said finally. "I'm in. But if you double-cross me, you'll regret it."

Lucas nodded, extending his hand. "Deal."

Individual Skills and Past Experiences

WITH THE TEAM ASSEMBLED, Lucas knew they had the potential to pull off the impossible. Each member brought something unique to the table, and their combined skills made them a formidable force.

Emma Hayes:

EMMA'S BACKGROUND IN computer science and engineering was unparalleled. She had graduated top of her class from MIT and quickly made a name for herself in the cybersecurity world. Her ability to hack into the most secure systems was legendary, and her moral compass, though unconventional, drove her to use her skills for what she deemed just causes.

Jack "Smooth" Taylor:

JACK'S LIFE OF CONS and scams had honed his abilities to read people and situations with uncanny accuracy. He could slip into any role, whether it be a high-rolling businessman or a down-on-his-luck gambler. His charm was his greatest weapon, able to win over even the most guarded individuals. His past experiences in the foster system had taught him resilience and adaptability, traits that made him indispensable to the team.

Carl "Tank" Johnson:

CARL'S MILITARY TRAINING had made him a force to be reckoned with. He was proficient in hand-to-hand combat, weapons, and tactical planning. His size and strength were intimidating, but it was his loyalty and sense of honor that made him reliable. Despite his rough exterior, Carl had a strong moral code and a deep sense of justice, often standing up for those who couldn't defend themselves.

The Team Begins to Bond

THE FIRST FEW MEETINGS were tense, as each member sized up the others. They were all used to working alone, relying solely on their own skills to get the job done. Trust was not easily earned, especially in their line of work. But Lucas knew that for the heist to succeed, they needed to function as a cohesive unit.

He organized a series of team-building exercises, disguised as strategy sessions. They practiced breaking into secure locations, running through scenarios that mirrored what they would face at Fort Knox. Slowly, the initial skepticism began to fade, replaced by a grudging respect for each other's abilities.

One evening, after a particularly grueling practice run, the team gathered around a fire pit outside their safe house. It was a rare moment of relaxation, the tension of the day easing with the warmth of the fire and the camaraderie that was beginning to form.

Lucas broke the silence. "We've all come from different backgrounds, but we share a common goal. We're here to prove that we can outsmart the system that's screwed us over. We've got the skills, and we've got the plan. All we need now is trust."

Emma nodded, her eyes reflecting the flames. "I've spent years fighting against corruption and greed. This is a chance to hit them where it hurts the most."

Jack smirked, taking a swig of his drink. "I've conned my way through life, but this... this is the ultimate con. I'm in for the thrill and the payoff."

Carl remained silent for a moment, then spoke, his deep voice carrying a weight of conviction. "I've seen the worst of what people can do to each other. If we can pull this off, it'll be a victory for all the little guys who've been crushed by the system."

Lucas looked at his team, feeling a sense of pride and determination. "We're not just doing this for the money. We're doing it to prove that we can. To show that no fortress is impregnable. To take back control of our lives."

As the night wore on, the team shared stories of their pasts, their struggles, and their dreams. They laughed and joked, the bonds of friendship beginning to form. It was in these moments that they found a common purpose, a shared sense of retribution against a world that had wronged them.

They were no longer just a group of individuals with a plan; they were a team, united by a shared goal and a burning desire to succeed. And as they sat around the fire, their determination solidified into a resolve that would carry them through the challenges ahead.

The heist was no longer just a plan on paper. It was their destiny, and they were ready to seize it.

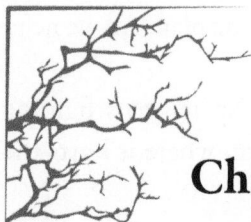

Chapter 3: Reconnaissance

The morning sun cast long shadows across the Kentucky landscape as the team gathered in a secluded cabin, miles away from Fort Knox. Lucas "Lucky" Kane stood at the head of the table, his sharp eyes scanning the room as he prepared to outline their next steps. Today marked the beginning of the reconnaissance phase—a critical part of the plan that would determine their success or failure.

"Alright, everyone," Lucas began, his voice steady and commanding. "This is where we start to gather the intel we need. Fort Knox is one of the most secure places in the world, but every fortress has its weak points. Our job is to find them."

The team nodded, their faces a mix of determination and anticipation. Emma Hayes, the tech genius, Jack "Smooth" Taylor, the con artist, and Carl "Tank" Johnson, the muscle, were all ready to put their skills to the test.

"First, we need to conduct detailed surveillance of the area," Lucas continued. "Emma, you'll be monitoring their electronic communications and hacking into their systems. Jack, you'll be on the ground, blending in and observing the guards and their routines. Carl, you and I will handle the physical reconnaissance and security analysis."

Emma was already setting up her laptop, her fingers flying over the keyboard. "I've got a list of frequencies and channels they use for their communications. I'll start monitoring them for any patterns or weaknesses."

Jack leaned back in his chair, a confident smile on his face. "I can get us the blueprints and insider info we need. Just point me in the right direction."

Carl cracked his knuckles, his intense gaze focused on Lucas. "Let's get started."

Detailed Surveillance

THE TEAM SPLIT INTO pairs, each with a specific task to accomplish. Lucas and Carl headed out to the perimeter of Fort Knox, a pair of high-powered binoculars and a camera with a telephoto lens in hand. They parked their unassuming SUV in a wooded area, far enough away to avoid suspicion but close enough to get a clear view of the facility.

Lucas peered through the binoculars, noting the high fences topped with razor wire, the heavily armed guards patrolling the grounds, and the numerous surveillance cameras strategically placed around the perimeter. He handed the binoculars to Carl, who began taking photos and documenting their observations.

"We're dealing with a layered security system here," Lucas said, jotting down notes. "The outer perimeter is the first line of defense, but it's the internal measures that will pose the real challenge."

Carl nodded, snapping photos of the guards and their patrol routes. "We need to figure out their rotation schedules and any blind spots in their coverage."

Meanwhile, Emma was back at the cabin, her laptop connected to a portable server. She had already managed to hack into the local power grid, giving her access to the area's electrical infrastructure. Now, she was working on tapping into Fort Knox's communication channels.

"Alright, I'm in," Emma said, her voice coming through the earpiece Lucas was wearing. "I've intercepted their radio frequencies. I'll monitor their communications and look for any patterns or vulnerabilities."

"Good work, Emma," Lucas replied. "Keep us updated on anything you find."

Jack, on the other hand, had adopted a different approach. He had disguised himself as a tourist, complete with a camera and a loud Hawaiian shirt. Fort Knox offered guided tours of certain areas to the public, and Jack intended to use this opportunity to gather valuable intel.

As he mingled with the other tourists, Jack's keen eyes observed the guards, noting their movements and interactions. He struck up conversations with the tour guides and other visitors, all the while gathering information and subtly probing for any useful details.

By the end of the day, the team reconvened at the cabin, ready to share their findings.

Analysis of Security Measures

LUCAS SPREAD A LARGE map of Fort Knox on the table, marking the locations of the guards, cameras, and other security features. Emma, Jack, and Carl gathered around, each contributing their observations.

"The outer perimeter is well-guarded, but I noticed a few potential weaknesses," Lucas began. "There's a section of the fence that seems to be under repair. It's still monitored by cameras, but it might be a way in if we can time it right."

Carl pointed to a series of photos he had taken. "I also noticed that the guards have a shift change every eight hours. There's a brief window during the transition where coverage is lighter."

Emma chimed in, "I've been monitoring their communications, and it seems like they have regular maintenance checks on their security systems. These checks create temporary blind spots in their camera coverage. If we can sync our movements with these checks, it could give us the time we need."

Jack leaned over the map, tracing a route with his finger. "I spoke to one of the tour guides and learned that they use a combination of biometric and keycard access for the internal doors. We'll need to get our hands on a keycard and a way to replicate the biometric data."

Lucas nodded, absorbing the information. "Good. Now, let's talk about the vault. It's the most secure part of the facility, and it's going to take everything we've got to breach it."

First Challenge: Obtaining Blueprints and Insider Information

TO SUCCESSFULLY PLAN their heist, the team needed detailed blueprints of Fort Knox and insider information about its security systems. Lucas had a contact in the black market who could potentially help, but it was a risky move. Trust was a rare commodity in their world, and relying on an outsider added an element of unpredictability.

Lucas decided to arrange a meeting with his contact, a man known only as "The Broker." He was an information dealer with connections in high places, and if anyone could get the blueprints, it was him.

The meeting was set in a dimly lit bar in a small town, far enough from Fort Knox to avoid suspicion. Lucas arrived early, taking a seat in a corner booth. He ordered a drink and waited, his eyes scanning the room for any signs of trouble.

A short, stocky man in a tailored suit entered the bar, his eyes hidden behind dark sunglasses. He approached Lucas's booth and slid into the seat opposite him.

"Lucas Kane," The Broker said, his voice low and gravelly. "I hear you're looking for something special."

Lucas nodded, leaning forward. "I need blueprints of Fort Knox. Detailed ones, including security measures and guard rotations."

The Broker raised an eyebrow. "That's a tall order. Fort Knox isn't exactly easy to penetrate."

"That's why I came to you," Lucas replied. "I know you have the connections to get what I need. Name your price."

The Broker chuckled. "Always straight to business. I like that. But this kind of information doesn't come cheap. I'll need a down payment upfront, and the rest upon delivery."

Lucas slid an envelope across the table. "Half now, half when you deliver."

The Broker opened the envelope, glanced at the stack of bills inside, and nodded. "You'll have your blueprints in three days. But be careful, Lucas. Fort Knox isn't a place to take lightly."

"I know what I'm doing," Lucas said, his voice steady. "Just get me the blueprints."

With the deal made, Lucas returned to the cabin, informing the team of the progress. In the meantime, they continued their surveillance and analysis, refining their plan with each new piece of information.

Emma Hacks into Government Databases

WHILE WAITING FOR THE blueprints, Emma focused on hacking into government databases to gather additional intel. She needed access to the security protocols and any recent changes to their systems. It was a high-risk move, but Emma was confident in her abilities.

Late at night, while the rest of the team slept, Emma sat at her laptop, her face illuminated by the glow of the screen. She had already bypassed several layers of security, but the final firewall was proving to be a challenge.

"Come on," she muttered, her fingers dancing over the keys. "Just a little more..."

Finally, with a triumphant beep, she was in. Emma quickly navigated the system, downloading files and extracting data. She found detailed information about the biometric security measures, the keycard access protocols, and the maintenance schedules.

"Got it," she whispered, a satisfied smile on her face.

Emma spent the next few hours analyzing the data, identifying potential weaknesses and opportunities. By the time dawn broke, she had compiled a comprehensive report, ready to present to the team.

The following morning, Lucas gathered everyone around the table. Emma handed out copies of her report, and the team reviewed the information.

"This is excellent work, Emma," Lucas said, impressed. "With this data, we can fine-tune our plan and increase our chances of success."

Emma nodded, her eyes bright with excitement. "I found a few key points we can exploit. The biometric system is updated every two weeks, and the next update is due right before our planned heist. If we can get in during that window, we can use the old data to our advantage."

Jack grinned. "Sounds like a plan. What about the keycards?"

"There's a maintenance worker who has access to most areas," Emma replied. "He's scheduled to be on-site during the maintenance checks. If we can get his keycard, it'll save us a lot of trouble."

Carl crossed his arms, his expression thoughtful. "How do we get close to him without raising suspicion?"

Jack's grin widened. "Leave that to me. I'll make sure he's more than willing to part with his keycard."

Lucas nodded, satisfied with the progress. "Alright, let's move forward with the next phase. We'll need to execute a dry run to ensure everything goes smoothly. Everyone

knows their roles. Let's make this happen."

Dry Run

THE DRY RUN WAS DESIGNED to test their plan in a controlled environment, ensuring that each team member knew their role and could execute it flawlessly. They had rented a warehouse and set up a mock version of Fort Knox, complete with simulated security measures and patrol routes.

Lucas watched as the team went through the motions, timing each step and noting any potential issues. Emma monitored the simulated security systems, Jack practiced acquiring the keycard and biometric data, and Carl ran through the physical infiltration.

Despite a few minor hiccups, the dry run was a success. The team worked seamlessly together, each member performing their role with precision and efficiency.

"Good work, everyone," Lucas said as they gathered for a debriefing. "We've identified a few areas to improve, but overall, we're on track. Let's address these issues and run through it again tomorrow."

The team nodded, their confidence growing with each practice run. They knew that the real heist would be infinitely more challenging, but these dry runs were essential to their preparation.

The Blueprints Arrive

THREE DAYS LATER, THE Broker delivered the blueprints as promised. Lucas spread them out on the table, and the team gathered around, studying the detailed schematics.

"These are exactly what we needed," Lucas said, a sense of satisfaction in his voice. "We now have a complete picture of Fort Knox's layout and security measures. Let's integrate this information into our plan."

Over the next few days, the team worked tirelessly, refining their strategy and addressing any potential weaknesses. They ran through multiple dry runs, each one smoother than the last, until they were confident in their ability to execute the heist.

Final Preparations

WITH THE RECONNAISSANCE complete and the plan finalized, the team began their final preparations. Emma fine-tuned her hacking tools, ensuring that everything was ready for the big day. Jack rehearsed his approach to the maintenance worker, perfecting his con. Carl maintained his physical training, ready to handle any obstacles that came their way.

Lucas, ever the strategist, reviewed every detail, running through the plan in his mind and anticipating any potential challenges. He knew that success depended on their ability to adapt and react to the unexpected, and he was determined to be ready for anything.

The night before the heist, Lucas called one final meeting. The team gathered around the table, their faces a mix of excitement and nerves.

"Tomorrow is the day," Lucas said, his voice steady. "We've planned and prepared for this moment. We know the risks, but we also know our strengths. Trust each other, stay focused, and we'll come out of this with the prize of a lifetime."

Emma nodded, her eyes shining with determination. "We've got this."

Jack grinned, his confidence unshaken. "I'm ready for the challenge."

Carl pounded his fist on the table. "Let's do this."

As they dispersed for the night, each team member felt a sense of anticipation and resolve. They had come together as a unit, each bringing their unique skills to the table. The reconnaissance phase had given them the information they needed, and now it was time to put their plan into action.

Lucas stood alone in the cabin, staring at the map of Fort Knox one last time. He knew that tomorrow would be the ultimate test of their abilities, but he also knew that they were ready. The pieces were in place, and the game was about to begin.

The heist of Fort Knox would be their greatest challenge, but with the team's skills and their meticulous planning, Lucas believed they could pull it off. As he turned off the lights and headed to bed, he felt a sense of calm and confidence. They were ready for whatever came their way.

Tomorrow, they would make history.

Chapter 4: The Inside Man

The sun was beginning to set, casting long shadows over the cabin where Lucas "Lucky" Kane and his team were gathered. Tonight, they would bring a new player into their scheme—someone who could provide the final piece of the puzzle. This player was Agent Tom Harris, a high-ranking security officer at Fort Knox. Lucas had a plan to coerce him into helping with the heist, but it wouldn't be easy.

"Alright, everyone," Lucas began, standing at the head of the table, "tonight we meet with Tom Harris. He's our key to getting inside Fort Knox. We need him to unlock the biometric and keycard systems."

Emma Hayes, the tech genius, looked up from her laptop. "How are we going to convince him to help us? He's not exactly going to be eager to betray Fort Knox."

"That's where the blackmail comes in," Lucas replied. "Tom has a few secrets he'd rather keep hidden. Jack, you'll be the one to make the initial contact. Your charm and ability to read people will be crucial."

Jack "Smooth" Taylor leaned back in his chair, a confident smile on his face. "I can handle that. What's his weakness?"

Lucas handed Jack a dossier on Tom Harris. "Tom has a gambling problem. He's racked up a lot of debt with some very dangerous people. If we threaten to expose him to his superiors and those he's in debt to, he'll have no choice but to help us."

Carl "Tank" Johnson, the muscle of the team, cracked his knuckles. "And if he doesn't cooperate?"

Lucas's eyes hardened. "Then we make him. But let's try to keep this as smooth as possible. We need him on our side, not just scared into compliance."

The team nodded in agreement. They knew the stakes were high, and bringing Tom Harris into their plan was a risky move, but it was necessary.

Introduction of Agent Tom Harris

AGENT TOM HARRIS WAS a man in his early forties, with a distinguished career in security. He had served in the military before transitioning to a high-ranking position at Fort Knox. His reputation was impeccable—loyal, dedicated, and incorruptible. But everyone has their breaking point, and for Tom, it was his gambling addiction.

Tom had started gambling as a way to unwind from the stresses of his job. What began as a harmless pastime quickly spiraled out of control. He found himself betting larger sums, chasing losses, and sinking deeper into debt. Despite his efforts to hide it, the debt had grown to a point where it threatened his career and personal life.

Lucas had uncovered Tom's gambling problem through a network of informants and digital sleuthing. He knew that Tom was on the edge, desperate for a way out. This desperation made him the perfect target for blackmail.

The Initial Contact

THE TEAM SET THEIR plan in motion, with Jack taking the lead. He arrived at a dimly lit bar in downtown Louisville, a known haunt of Tom's. Jack had carefully chosen this location for its privacy and the likelihood that Tom would be there.

Jack spotted Tom at the bar, nursing a drink. He approached casually, taking a seat next to him. "Mind if I join you?"

Tom glanced at Jack, his eyes wary. "It's a free country."

Jack ordered a drink and turned to Tom. "You look like a man with a lot on his mind."

Tom grunted, taking a sip of his whiskey. "You could say that."

Jack leaned in slightly, lowering his voice. "I've got a proposition that could help with your... problem."

Tom stiffened, his grip tightening on his glass. "I don't know what you're talking about."

Jack smiled, a hint of steel in his eyes. "Sure you do. Gambling debts, right? You're in deep with some very dangerous people."

Tom's eyes widened, panic flashing across his face. "Who are you?"

"Someone who can help," Jack replied smoothly. "But you'll have to do something for me in return."

Tom shook his head, his voice trembling. "I can't... I can't do anything illegal. My job, my career—"

"Your career will be the least of your worries if those debt collectors find you," Jack interrupted. "Think about it, Tom. I'm offering you a way out. No more debt, no more fear."

Tom stared into his drink, the weight of his situation pressing down on him. Finally, he nodded, his voice barely above a whisper. "What do you need me to do?"

Leveraging Tom's Position

JACK RELAYED THE DETAILS of the conversation to the team. They gathered in the cabin, discussing the next steps.

"Tom's in," Jack said, a satisfied smile on his face. "He's scared, but he's willing to cooperate."

Lucas nodded. "Good. Now we need to leverage his position to our advantage. Emma, what can you do with the access he'll provide?"

Emma's eyes gleamed with anticipation. "Once we have his keycard and biometric data, I can hack into the security systems and disable the alarms and cameras for a short period. We'll need precise timing, but it's doable."

Lucas turned to Carl. "You'll be our enforcer. Make sure Tom stays in line and doesn't try anything funny."

Carl grinned, cracking his knuckles. "Consider it done."

Tom's Personal Stakes and Internal Conflict

TOM HARRIS SAT IN HIS small, cluttered apartment, staring at the stack of bills and threatening letters piled on his kitchen table. He felt trapped, suffocated by the weight of his debts and the knowledge that his career—and possibly his life—were on the line. The encounter with Jack had shaken him, but it also offered a glimmer of hope. If he helped them, he could rid himself of the crushing debt and start anew. But the thought of betraying Fort Knox, his colleagues, and everything he stood for filled him with dread.

As a young man, Tom had joined the military to serve his country, driven by a deep sense of duty and honor. His years of service had been marked by bravery and dedication, earning him commendations and respect. Transitioning to a civilian role at Fort Knox had seemed like a natural progression—a way to continue serving and protecting his nation's most valuable assets. The idea of betraying that trust was anathema to him.

Tom poured himself a drink, hoping to steady his nerves. He knew he was in over his head, but the fear of what would happen if he didn't cooperate with Jack and his team was even greater. The debt collectors had already started making threats, and he couldn't risk them following through.

He was torn between his oath and his survival, between his honor and his desperation. The internal conflict gnawed at him, keeping him awake at night and haunting his thoughts during the day. The more he thought about it, the more he realized he had no choice. He had to go through with it, but he vowed to himself that he would find a way to make things right once it was all over.

Strategy Sessions

LUCAS CALLED ANOTHER meeting at the cabin to finalize their strategy with Tom's involvement. The team gathered around the table, each member focused and ready.

"Tom has agreed to help us," Lucas began. "But we need to ensure he follows through. Emma, what's our next step?"

Emma pulled up a schematic of Fort Knox on her laptop. "We need to get Tom's keycard and biometric data. Once we have that, I can create duplicates and set up remote access to the security systems."

Lucas nodded. "Jack, you'll handle the keycard. Carl, you'll ensure Tom stays in line. Let's run through the plan."

Jack and Carl listened intently as Emma outlined the technical details. Lucas added his insights, ensuring that every aspect was covered. They rehearsed their roles, fine-tuning the plan until everyone was confident.

The next step was to meet with Tom and get what they needed. The team set up a secure location for the meeting—a secluded warehouse on the outskirts of the city. It was here that they would collect the keycard and biometric data and ensure Tom's cooperation.

The Meeting with Tom

TOM ARRIVED AT THE warehouse, his heart pounding in his chest. He felt like a man walking to his execution, but he reminded himself that this was his only way out. He was greeted by Lucas, Jack, and Carl, their expressions serious.

"Tom," Lucas said, extending a hand. "Thank you for meeting us."

Tom shook his hand, trying to steady his nerves. "Let's get this over with."

Lucas led him to a table where Emma was set up with her equipment. "We need your keycard and a scan of your fingerprint and retina. Emma will handle the technical side."

Tom handed over his keycard, feeling a pang of guilt as he did. Emma took it and began scanning it into her laptop. She then directed Tom to a small device that would capture his biometric data.

"Just look into the scanner," Emma instructed. "It'll only take a moment."

Tom complied, feeling a sense of resignation wash over him. Once the scans were complete, Emma nodded to Lucas. "We're all set."

Lucas turned to Tom. "You've done your part. Now we need you to stick to your routine and act normal. If anyone gets suspicious, this whole thing falls apart."

Tom nodded, feeling the weight of his decision. "I understand."

Carl stepped forward, his imposing presence adding to the gravity of the situation. "Remember, Tom, we're watching. If you try anything, we'll know."

Tom swallowed hard, the fear in his eyes evident. "I won't. I just want this to be over."

Lucas placed a reassuring hand on Tom's shoulder. "It will be. Just do as we've discussed, and you'll be free of your debts. We'll contact you with further instructions."

Tom left the warehouse, feeling a mix of relief and dread. He knew he was in too deep to back out now, and all he could do was follow through and hope for the best.

The Team's Strategy to Leverage Tom's Position

WITH TOM'S KEYCARD and biometric data in hand, the team set about integrating this new intel into their plan. Emma worked tirelessly, programming the duplicates and setting up remote access to the Fort Knox security systems. She created a series of scripts that would allow her to override the alarms and cameras for a limited time, synchronized with their infiltration.

Lucas and Jack focused on refining their approach. They knew that timing was crucial, and any deviation from the plan could spell disaster. They rehearsed their roles, ensuring that every move was precise and coordinated.

Carl continued his training, ready to handle any physical obstacles that might arise. His role as the enforcer was critical, and he needed to be prepared for anything.

The team held regular strategy sessions, discussing every detail and potential contingency. They knew that the success of their heist depended on their ability to adapt and react to the unexpected.

"We need to be ready for anything," Lucas emphasized during one of their meetings. "If something goes wrong, we need to be able to pivot and keep moving."

Emma nodded, her eyes focused on her laptop screen. "I've set up a series of backup scripts in case we encounter any issues. But we need to stick to the plan as closely as possible."

Jack grinned, his confidence unwavering. "We've got this. We've planned for every scenario."

Carl cracked his knuckles, his expression determined. "Just say the word, boss."

Lucas felt a sense of pride and determination. They had come a long way, and they were ready for the challenge. The heist was within their grasp, and with Tom's help, they had a real shot at pulling it off.

Tom's Internal Conflict Deepens

AS THE DAY OF THE HEIST approached, Tom's internal conflict grew more intense. He struggled with the knowledge that he was betraying his colleagues and everything he had worked for. The guilt gnawed at him, and he found it increasingly difficult to sleep.

He spent hours going over the plan in his mind, trying to find a way to fulfill his part without compromising his principles. But every time he thought about backing out, the fear of the debt collectors and the consequences of his actions kept him in line.

Tom tried to maintain a façade of normalcy at work, but his colleagues noticed a change in him. He was more withdrawn, more anxious. Some attributed it to the pressures of the job, but a few began to suspect that something was amiss.

One evening, as Tom was leaving work, his supervisor, Captain Mark Dawson, called him into his office. Mark was a stern but fair man, respected by his subordinates.

"Tom, sit down," Mark said, gesturing to a chair. "I've noticed you've been a bit off lately. Is everything alright?"

Tom forced a smile, trying to hide his unease. "Just a lot on my plate, sir. Nothing I can't handle."

Mark studied him for a moment, his gaze piercing. "You've been one of my best officers, Tom. If there's something going on, you can talk to me. We can find a way to help."

Tom's heart raced, the weight of his secrets pressing down on him. He knew he couldn't confide in Mark, but the genuine concern in his voice made him question his decisions even more.

"Thank you, sir," Tom said finally. "But I'm fine. Just dealing with some personal issues. I appreciate your concern."

Mark nodded, but the look in his eyes told Tom that he wasn't convinced. "Alright, Tom. But remember, my door is always open."

Tom left the office, feeling more conflicted than ever. He knew he was walking a tightrope, and any misstep could lead to disaster.

The Final Preparations

THE TEAM CONTINUED their preparations, each member focused on their role. Emma fine-tuned her scripts, ensuring that everything was ready for the big day. Jack rehearsed his approach, perfecting his con. Carl maintained his physical training, ready to handle any obstacles.

Lucas kept a close eye on Tom, monitoring his movements and communications. He knew that the success of their heist depended on Tom's cooperation, and he needed to ensure that everything went smoothly.

The night before the heist, Lucas called one final meeting. The team gathered around the table, their faces a mix of excitement and nerves.

"Tomorrow is the day," Lucas said, his voice steady. "We've planned and prepared for this moment. We know the risks, but we also know our strengths. Trust each other, stay focused, and we'll come out of this with the prize of a lifetime."

Emma nodded, her eyes shining with determination. "We've got this."

Jack grinned, his confidence unshaken. "I'm ready for the challenge."

Carl pounded his fist on the table. "Let's do this."

As they dispersed for the night, each team member felt a sense of anticipation and resolve. They had come together as a unit, each bringing their unique skills to the table. The reconnaissance phase had given them the information they needed, and now it was time to put their plan into action.

Lucas stood alone in the cabin, staring at the map of Fort Knox one last time. He knew that tomorrow would be the ultimate test of their abilities, but he also knew that they were ready. The pieces were in place, and the game was about to begin.

The heist of Fort Knox would be their greatest challenge, but with the team's skills and their meticulous planning, Lucas believed they could pull it off. As he turned off the lights and headed to bed, he felt a sense of calm and confidence. They were ready for whatever came their way.

Tomorrow, they would make history.

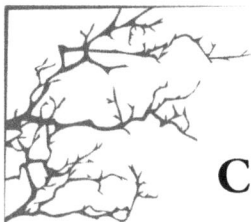

Chapter 5: The Dry Run

The sun rose over the Kentucky hills, casting a golden hue over the secluded warehouse the team had converted into their training ground. Lucas "Lucky" Kane stood in the center of the space, his sharp eyes scanning the area as he mentally reviewed the day's agenda. Today was the day for their dry run—a full-scale practice of the heist. This was the culmination of weeks of planning, reconnaissance, and preparation.

"Alright, everyone," Lucas called out, gathering his team. "Today, we practice the heist from start to finish. This dry run will test our plan, our timing, and our ability to work together under pressure. Treat it like the real thing, because if we can't get it right here, we won't get it right when it matters."

Emma Hayes, the tech genius, was already setting up her laptop and equipment. Jack "Smooth" Taylor, the con artist, adjusted his disguise in a mirror, his face reflecting a mixture of confidence and anticipation. Carl "Tank" Johnson, the muscle, did a final check of his gear, his imposing figure radiating readiness.

Lucas laid out a detailed map of their mock setup, a meticulously crafted replica of Fort Knox, complete with fences, cameras, and guard stations. He pointed to various points on the map, assigning roles and explaining the sequence of events.

"Emma, you'll handle the security systems. Your job is to disable the alarms and cameras, giving us a window to move. Jack, you're our infiltrator. You'll use your charm and skills to gain access and acquire the keycard and biometric data. Carl, you're on crowd control and physical security. Make sure no one interferes with our operation."

The team nodded, each member focused on their role. Lucas continued, "We need to be in and out in under 30 minutes. Precision and timing are everything. Let's do this."

Role Assignments and Synchronization of Tasks

THE DRY RUN BEGAN WITH Emma setting up her hacking station near the perimeter of their mock Fort Knox. She had a series of scripts ready to override the security systems, and she worked quickly, her fingers flying over the keyboard.

"I'm in," Emma announced, her voice steady. "Disabling cameras and alarms now. You have a five-minute window."

Jack slipped into his role as an undercover agent, his demeanor shifting to match his fabricated persona. He approached the main entrance, greeting the simulated guards with a charming smile.

"Morning, gentlemen," Jack said, flashing a fake ID. "I'm here for a security audit."

The guards, played by Lucas and Carl, nodded and allowed him to pass. Jack moved swiftly, making his way to the office where the keycard and biometric data were stored. He retrieved the keycard and used a small device to scan his fingerprint and retina, replicating the necessary data for their heist.

"Got the goods," Jack reported through his earpiece. "Heading to the rendezvous point."

Meanwhile, Carl was stationed near the main hall, keeping an eye on the mock guards and ensuring no one interfered with Jack's mission. His presence was intimidating, and he easily handled any simulated threats.

Lucas coordinated the operation from the control room, monitoring the team's progress and timing each step. "We're on schedule," he said. "Everyone, stay sharp and stick to the plan."

As the team converged at the rendezvous point, Emma provided real-time updates on the security system's status. "Cameras and alarms will reboot in two minutes," she warned. "We need to move fast."

Mistakes and Tensions

DESPITE THEIR METICULOUS planning, a few mistakes occurred during the dry run. Jack's fake ID was almost detected by the guards, and he had to think quickly to avoid suspicion. Emma's scripts took longer to execute than anticipated, cutting their window dangerously close. Carl's handling of a simulated threat was slightly delayed, causing a brief but tense moment.

The team regrouped at the warehouse, the air thick with tension. Lucas could see the frustration and anxiety in their eyes, and he knew they needed to address these issues before the real heist.

"Alright, let's debrief," Lucas said, gathering everyone around the table. "What went wrong?"

Emma spoke first, her voice tight with frustration. "My scripts took longer to run than expected. I'll need to streamline the code and run more tests."

Jack nodded, still fuming from his close call. "My fake ID was almost compromised. We need a better backstory and more convincing documents."

Carl, always the pragmatist, added, "I hesitated for a second when dealing with that threat. I need to be quicker and more decisive."

Lucas listened carefully, his mind racing with solutions. "We've identified the problems, now let's fix them. Emma, streamline your scripts and run more simulations. Jack, we'll work on a more solid backstory and improve the fake documents. Carl, practice your response times. We need to be perfect."

Despite their agreement, the tension was palpable. The pressure of the upcoming heist weighed heavily on everyone, and the mistakes during the dry run had shaken their confidence.

Emphasizing Precision and Unity

LUCAS KNEW HE HAD TO address the underlying tension and rebuild the team's confidence. He called for a break and led the team outside to a nearby clearing. The fresh air and change of scenery helped to clear their minds.

"Look," Lucas began, his tone calm but firm, "I know today didn't go perfectly. But that's why we're doing these dry runs—to find the flaws and fix them before the real thing. We're a team, and we need to support each other."

Emma nodded, her frustration easing. "You're right. We've come too far to let a few mistakes derail us."

Jack sighed, his anger dissipating. "Yeah, I guess I overreacted. We'll get it right next time."

Carl, ever the steady presence, simply said, "We've got this. We just need to stay focused."

Lucas continued, "We need precision and unity. Every second counts, and we can't afford any hesitation or miscommunication. Trust in your skills and trust in each other. We've planned for every scenario, and we're ready. We just need to execute."

The team nodded, their resolve strengthened. They returned to the warehouse, ready to run through the dry run again, this time with renewed focus and determination.

Refining the Plan

EMMA SPENT THE NEXT few hours refining her scripts, cutting down the execution time and running multiple tests to ensure everything worked smoothly. Jack and Lucas worked on creating a more convincing backstory for his undercover role, including forged documents and a detailed personal history.

Carl practiced his response times, running through various scenarios and improving his reaction speed. The team ran through the dry run several more times, each iteration smoother and more precise.

By the end of the day, they had ironed out the major issues and were functioning like a well-oiled machine. Lucas called for another debriefing, this time with a sense of accomplishment in the air.

"Great work, everyone," Lucas said, a rare smile on his face. "We've made significant progress, and I'm confident we're ready for the real thing. Just remember, precision and unity. We succeed together, or we fail together."

Emma, Jack, and Carl nodded, their confidence restored. They knew the stakes were high, but they also knew they had the skills and the plan to pull it off.

The Final Dry Run

THE NEXT MORNING, THE team gathered for one final dry run. This would be their last practice before the actual heist, and they were determined to make it flawless.

Emma set up her equipment, her movements confident and precise. "I'm in," she announced. "Disabling cameras and alarms now. You have a five-minute window."

Jack slipped into his undercover role, his disguise and backstory now flawless. He approached the main entrance, greeting the guards with his usual charm.

"Morning, gentlemen," Jack said, flashing his improved fake ID. "I'm here for a security audit."

The guards nodded and allowed him to pass. Jack moved swiftly, making his way to the office and retrieving the keycard and biometric data. He reported his success through his earpiece and headed to the rendezvous point.

Carl maintained his position near the main hall, ready to handle any threats. His improved response times and decisive actions ensured that no one interfered with Jack's mission.

Lucas coordinated the operation from the control room, monitoring the team's progress and timing each step. "We're on schedule," he said. "Everyone, stay sharp and stick to the plan."

As the team converged at the rendezvous point, Emma provided real-time updates on the security system's status. "Cameras and alarms will reboot in two minutes," she warned. "We need to move fast."

This time, everything went smoothly. The team completed the dry run within the allotted time, their movements precise and coordinated.

Post-Run Debrief

LUCAS GATHERED THE team for a final debriefing, a sense of satisfaction in the air. "Excellent work, everyone. We've ironed out the kinks and are ready for the real thing. Let's go over the plan one last time."

Emma presented her refined scripts, explaining how she would disable the security systems and provide real-time updates. Jack detailed his undercover role and how he would acquire the keycard and biometric data. Carl reviewed his position and how he would handle any threats.

Lucas nodded, pleased with their progress. "We've planned for every scenario and practiced until we're perfect. Tomorrow, we put it all into action. Remember, precision and unity. We succeed together, or we fail together."

The team nodded, their confidence unwavering. They knew the stakes were high, but they also knew they had the skills and the plan to pull it off.

The Night Before

AS THE TEAM PREPARED for bed, Lucas took a moment to reflect on their journey. They had come a long way, and he felt a deep sense of pride in their progress. He knew the heist would be their greatest challenge, but he also knew they were ready.

Lucas gathered everyone in the common area, a final moment of unity before the big day. "Tomorrow, we make history. We've worked hard and planned meticulously. Trust in your skills and trust in each other. We've got this."

Emma, Jack, and Carl nodded, their resolve strengthened. They knew the stakes were high, but they also knew they had the skills and the plan to pull it off.

As they headed to bed, each team member felt a sense of anticipation and resolve. They had come together as a unit, each bringing their unique skills to the table. The dry run had given them the confidence they needed, and now it was time to put their plan into action.

Lucas stood alone in the common area, staring at the map of Fort Knox one last time. He knew that tomorrow would be the ultimate test of their abilities, but he also knew that they were ready. The pieces were in place, and the game was about to begin.

The heist of Fort Knox would be their greatest challenge, but with the team's skills and their meticulous planning, Lucas believed they could pull it off. As he turned off the lights and headed to bed, he felt a sense of calm and confidence. They were ready for whatever came their way.

Tomorrow, they would make history.

Execution Day

THE MORNING OF THE heist arrived, and the team gathered at their designated meeting point, a secluded spot near Fort Knox. The air was charged with anticipation and nerves. They were about to embark on the most ambitious heist of their careers, and every detail needed to be perfect.

Lucas addressed the team one final time. "This is it. We've planned, we've practiced, and now it's time to execute. Remember, precision and unity. We succeed together, or we fail together. Trust in your skills and trust in each other. Let's make history."

Emma set up her equipment, ready to disable the security systems. "I'm in position and ready to go."

Jack adjusted his disguise and took a deep breath, slipping into his undercover persona. "Ready to roll."

Carl checked his gear one last time, his expression focused and determined. "I'm ready."

Lucas nodded, feeling a surge of pride and determination. "Let's do this."

The Heist Begins

THE TEAM MOVED INTO position, each member executing their role with precision and confidence. Emma disabled the cameras and alarms, creating a five-minute window for Jack to gain access. Jack approached the main entrance, his fake ID and backstory now flawless. He greeted the guards with his usual charm and was allowed to pass.

Inside, Jack moved swiftly, retrieving the keycard and biometric data with ease. He reported his success and headed to the rendezvous point. Carl maintained his position, ready to handle any threats.

Lucas monitored the operation from the control room, coordinating the team's movements and ensuring everything stayed on schedule. "We're on track. Everyone, stay sharp and stick to the plan."

As the team converged at the rendezvous point, Emma provided real-time updates on the security system's status. "Cameras and alarms will reboot in two minutes. We need to move fast."

The team moved with precision and coordination, each step executed flawlessly. They reached the vault, and Emma used the keycard and biometric data to gain access. The vault door opened, revealing the vast reserves of gold inside.

Lucas felt a surge of triumph. They had done it. They had breached Fort Knox.

The Escape

WITH THE GOLD SECURED, the team began their escape. They moved quickly and efficiently, each member playing their role to perfection. Emma monitored the security systems, ensuring they had enough time to get out before the alarms reactivated. Jack and Carl handled any obstacles, their actions smooth and decisive.

Lucas coordinated their movements, keeping everyone on track and focused. "We're almost there. Keep moving."

As they reached the exit, the alarms began to blare. Emma had timed it perfectly, giving them just enough time to escape before the security systems fully reactivated.

The team made their way to their getaway vehicles, the adrenaline pumping through their veins. They had done it. They had pulled off the heist of a lifetime.

The Aftermath

BACK AT THE SAFE HOUSE, the team celebrated their success. They had faced countless challenges and overcome them all, their skills and teamwork carrying them through.

Lucas gathered everyone around the table, a rare smile on his face. "We did it. We pulled off the impossible. I'm proud of each and every one of you."

Emma, Jack, and Carl nodded, their faces reflecting a mixture of relief and triumph. They had made history, and they had done it together.

As they divided the spoils and prepared to go their separate ways, Lucas felt a deep sense of satisfaction. They had achieved their goal, and they had done it with precision and unity.

The heist of Fort Knox would go down in history as one of the greatest heists ever pulled off. And it was all thanks to their meticulous planning, unwavering determination, and unbreakable trust in each other.

As the team disbanded, each member heading off to their new lives, Lucas couldn't help but feel a sense of anticipation for the future. They had proven that they were capable of anything, and he knew that whatever challenges lay ahead, they would face them together.

They had made history, and they were ready for whatever came next.

Chapter 6: Security Breach

The morning light streamed through the windows of the cabin, casting long shadows on the faces of Lucas "Lucky" Kane and his team. Today was a critical day in their elaborate heist plan. They were about to take on one of the most critical and dangerous parts of the operation: creating a temporary blackout at Fort Knox. Lucas stood at the head of the table, his eyes scanning the room as he addressed his team.

"Today, we take a closer look at Fort Knox's security system," Lucas began. "Emma, you've done extensive research on their electronic defenses. Walk us through what we're dealing with."

Emma Hayes, the tech genius of the team, stepped forward. Her auburn hair was tied back, and her eyes were bright with intensity. She tapped a few keys on her laptop, and a detailed schematic of Fort Knox's security system appeared on the screen behind her.

"Fort Knox has a multi-layered security system that's virtually impenetrable," Emma explained. "They have motion detectors, infrared sensors, biometric locks, and a state-of-the-art alarm system. But the backbone of their security is their power grid. If we can disrupt that, we can create a window of opportunity."

Jack "Smooth" Taylor, the con artist, leaned back in his chair, a skeptical look on his face. "A window of opportunity? How long are we talking about here?"

Emma continued, "During a power outage, their systems will switch to backup generators, which have a five-second delay. It's a small window, but it's enough for us to exploit if we're precise."

Carl "Tank" Johnson, the muscle, cracked his knuckles. "So, how do we create this blackout?"

Emma pulled up another schematic, this time of a local power station. "We need to infiltrate this power station and plant a device that will cause a temporary blackout at Fort Knox. It's heavily guarded, and we'll need to move quickly and efficiently."

Lucas nodded, his mind racing with the details. "Alright, everyone. This is a crucial part of our plan. We need to execute it flawlessly. Emma, you'll handle the technical side. Jack and Carl, you'll assist with the infiltration. Let's go over the plan in detail."

A Closer Look at Fort Knox's Security System

FORT KNOX WAS KNOWN as one of the most secure places in the world, and for good reason. The facility's security system was a marvel of modern technology, designed to thwart any attempt at unauthorized access. As Emma detailed the various layers of security, the team listened intently, understanding the gravity of the challenge ahead.

"First, we have the outer perimeter," Emma began, pointing to the schematic. "It's surrounded by a high fence topped with razor wire. The fence is electrified and monitored by surveillance cameras and motion sensors."

Lucas interjected, "We'll need to disable the cameras and sensors before we can even think about getting close."

Emma nodded. "Exactly. Once we're past the fence, we'll encounter infrared sensors that detect body heat. These are spread throughout the grounds and are connected to the main security hub inside the facility."

Jack whistled low. "They really don't want anyone getting in, do they?"

Emma smiled wryly. "No, they don't. Inside the building, we have biometric locks on all the main doors. These require both a retinal scan and a fingerprint. The vault itself is surrounded by solid granite walls and an alarm system that's triggered by any unauthorized access."

Carl crossed his arms, his expression grim. "Sounds like a fortress."

"It is," Emma replied. "But every fortress has its weak points. The key is the power grid. If we can disrupt it, we create that crucial five-second window where their systems switch to backup power. That's when we make our move."

Emma Devises a Plan to Create a Temporary Blackout

THE TEAM GATHERED AROUND Emma as she explained her plan to create a temporary blackout at Fort Knox. The power station that supplied electricity to Fort Knox was located several miles away, heavily guarded and monitored.

"We need to plant a device at the power station that will cause a temporary outage," Emma explained. "This device will be programmed to activate at a specific time, causing a brief but significant power loss."

Lucas leaned forward, his eyes narrowing. "What kind of device are we talking about?"

Emma pulled out a small, sleek gadget from her bag. "This is an EMP generator. It's designed to emit a short burst of electromagnetic pulse that will disrupt the power grid temporarily. It's powerful enough to cause a blackout but short enough to avoid long-term damage."

Jack raised an eyebrow. "And you're sure this will work?"

Emma nodded confidently. "I've run multiple simulations. As long as we place it correctly and activate it at the right time, it will work."

Carl examined the device, his face serious. "What's the plan for getting this thing inside the power station?"

Emma brought up a blueprint of the power station. "We'll need to infiltrate the station, bypass the security systems, and plant the device near the main transformer. The station is guarded, but I've identified a few potential entry points."

Lucas studied the blueprint, his mind working through the logistics. "Alright. Jack, you'll handle the guards and any personnel inside. Carl, you'll provide backup and deal with any physical obstacles. Emma, you'll plant the device. I'll coordinate from the control room."

The Infiltration of the Power Station

THE TEAM PREPARED FOR the mission, each member focused on their role. They knew the risks involved and the importance of success. Failure was not an option.

That night, they set out for the power station in a nondescript van, equipped with the tools and gear they needed. The drive was tense, each member lost in their thoughts, preparing for the task ahead.

As they approached the power station, Lucas directed the team to park the van a safe distance away. They moved on foot, using the cover of darkness to approach the facility.

"Stay sharp," Lucas whispered through their earpieces. "Emma, you're up first."

Emma nodded, her hands steady as she set up her hacking equipment. She quickly bypassed the outer security system, disabling the cameras and motion sensors.

"Camera feeds are down," Emma reported. "We have a clear path to the main gate."

Jack took the lead, his movements smooth and confident. He approached the main gate, using a set of lock-picking tools to bypass the lock. Within moments, the gate swung open, and the team slipped inside.

They moved quickly and silently, navigating the maze of machinery and equipment inside the power station. Emma directed them towards the main transformer, the heart of the facility's power grid.

As they approached the transformer, a guard appeared around the corner. Jack acted swiftly, his charm and quick thinking coming into play.

"Hey there," Jack said, flashing a fake ID. "We're with the maintenance crew, here for a routine check."

The guard looked skeptical but didn't raise an alarm. "I wasn't informed of any maintenance work tonight."

Jack smiled, his demeanor friendly. "It was a last-minute request. We'll be in and out before you know it."

The guard nodded reluctantly, allowing them to pass. Jack and Carl exchanged a glance, relieved that the encounter had gone smoothly.

Emma reached the transformer and began setting up the EMP device. She worked quickly, her hands moving with practiced precision. Carl stood guard, keeping an eye out for any other personnel.

"Almost done," Emma said, her voice steady. "Just a few more adjustments."

Challenges and Obstacles

JUST AS EMMA WAS FINISHING up, another guard appeared, this one more alert and suspicious than the first. He approached Carl, his hand hovering near his holster.

"What are you doing here?" the guard demanded, his eyes narrowing.

Carl stepped forward, his imposing presence meant to intimidate. "Maintenance work. Got a problem with that?"

The guard's hand moved to his holster, his suspicion growing. "I wasn't informed of any maintenance work. I need to see some ID."

Jack stepped in, his voice calm and authoritative. "We're on a tight schedule. If you have an issue, take it up with management. Otherwise, let us do our job."

The guard hesitated, clearly torn. Sensing the situation escalating, Lucas spoke through their earpieces.

"Jack, handle this. We can't afford any delays."

Jack nodded subtly, turning his full attention to the guard. "Look, we're just trying to do our job. If you want to call it in, go ahead. But it's going to delay everything and you'll be the one answering to your superiors."

The guard seemed to waver, his hand still on his holster. Just as the tension reached its peak, a noise from the back of the station drew his attention. It was a fortunate distraction, and the guard turned away, muttering something under his breath.

"Let's wrap this up," Lucas urged. "We don't have much time."

Emma finished setting up the EMP device and activated a timer. "The device is set. We have ten minutes to get out of here before it goes off."

The team moved quickly, retracing their steps back to the main gate. They slipped out into the night, their hearts pounding with adrenaline. Once outside the gate, they made their way back to the van, breathing a collective sigh of relief as they drove away from the power station.

The Aftermath

BACK AT THE CABIN, the team gathered to debrief and ensure everything was set for the next phase of their plan. Emma pulled up the timer on her laptop, showing the countdown to the EMP activation.

"We did it," Emma said, a note of triumph in her voice. "The device is in place and will activate as planned."

Lucas nodded, a sense of satisfaction in his eyes. "Good work, everyone. We've cleared a major hurdle. Now, we need to focus on the heist itself."

Jack leaned back in his chair, a grin spreading across his face. "That was intense, but we pulled it off."

Carl nodded, his expression serious. "We need to stay sharp. This was just one part of the plan. The real challenge is still ahead."

Lucas addressed the team, his voice firm and confident. "We've shown that we can handle the pressure and overcome obstacles. We need to maintain this level of focus and precision. The blackout will give us the opportunity we need, but we have to be ready to move quickly and efficiently."

Emma reviewed the technical aspects of the EMP device, ensuring that everything was set for the blackout. "Once the blackout occurs, we'll have a five-second window to make our move. We need to be in position and ready to go."

Lucas outlined the next steps, detailing the sequence of events and each team member's role. "Jack, you'll handle the guards and personnel inside Fort Knox. Carl, you'll provide backup and deal with any physical obstacles. Emma, you'll manage the security systems and provide real-time updates. I'll coordinate from the control room."

The team nodded, each member focused and ready. They knew the stakes were high, and they were determined to succeed.

Preparing for the Heist

THE NEXT FEW DAYS WERE a whirlwind of preparation and final adjustments. The team ran through simulations and rehearsed their roles, fine-tuning every detail to ensure a flawless execution.

Lucas maintained a close watch on the countdown timer, coordinating with Emma to ensure the EMP device was functioning correctly. He knew that timing was crucial, and any deviation could jeopardize the entire operation.

Jack and Carl continued their training, refining their techniques and ensuring they were ready for any challenges that might arise. They knew that the success of the heist depended on their ability to handle the unexpected and adapt quickly.

Emma ran multiple tests on her scripts, ensuring that the security systems would be disabled as planned. She also set up backup scripts in case of any unforeseen issues, determined to leave nothing to chance.

The night before the heist, Lucas called one final meeting. The team gathered around the table, their faces reflecting a mix of anticipation and nerves.

"Tomorrow is the day," Lucas said, his voice steady. "We've planned and prepared for this moment. We know the risks, but we also know our strengths. Trust in your skills and trust in each other. We've got this."

Emma nodded, her eyes shining with determination. "We've come too far to back down now."

Jack grinned, his confidence unwavering. "I'm ready for the challenge."

Carl pounded his fist on the table. "Let's do this."

As they dispersed for the night, each team member felt a sense of anticipation and resolve. They had come together as a unit, each bringing their unique skills to the table. The mission to the power station had given them the confidence they needed, and now it was time to put their plan into action.

The Day of the Heist

THE MORNING OF THE heist arrived, and the team gathered at their designated meeting point, a secluded spot near Fort Knox. The air was charged with anticipation and nerves. They were about to embark on the most ambitious heist of their careers, and every detail needed to be perfect.

Lucas addressed the team one final time. "This is it. We've planned, we've practiced, and now it's time to execute. Remember, precision and unity. We succeed together, or we fail together. Trust in your skills and trust in each other. Let's make history."

Emma set up her equipment, ready to disable the security systems. "I'm in position and ready to go."

Jack adjusted his disguise and took a deep breath, slipping into his undercover persona. "Ready to roll."

Carl checked his gear one last time, his expression focused and determined. "I'm ready."

Lucas nodded, feeling a surge of pride and determination. "Let's do this."

The Blackout

AS THE COUNTDOWN TIMER approached zero, the team moved into position. Emma monitored the EMP device, ensuring that everything was set for the blackout. The tension was palpable, each member focused and ready.

"Three minutes to blackout," Emma announced. "Everyone, get ready."

Jack and Carl moved into position, ready to make their move as soon as the blackout occurred. Lucas coordinated their movements, keeping everyone on track and focused.

"One minute to blackout," Emma said, her voice steady.

The team held their breath, the anticipation building. As the timer hit zero, the EMP device activated, sending a burst of electromagnetic pulse through the power grid.

"Blackout in effect," Emma reported. "We have five seconds. Move!"

Jack and Carl moved swiftly, using the cover of darkness to slip past the outer perimeter. Emma disabled the security systems, providing real-time updates to the team.

"Alarms and cameras are down," Emma said. "You have a clear path."

The team moved with precision and coordination, each step executed flawlessly. They reached the vault, and Emma used the keycard and biometric data to gain access. The vault door opened, revealing the vast reserves of gold inside.

Lucas felt a surge of triumph. They had done it. They had breached Fort Knox.

The Escape

WITH THE GOLD SECURED, the team began their escape. They moved quickly and efficiently, each member playing their role to perfection. Emma monitored the security systems, ensuring they had enough time to get out before the alarms reactivated. Jack and Carl handled any obstacles, their actions smooth and decisive.

Lucas coordinated their movements, keeping everyone on track and focused. "We're almost there. Keep moving."

As they reached the exit, the alarms began to blare. Emma had timed it perfectly, giving them just enough time to escape before the security systems fully reactivated.

The team made their way to their getaway vehicles, the adrenaline pumping through their veins. They had done it. They had pulled off the heist of a lifetime.

The Aftermath

BACK AT THE SAFE HOUSE, the team celebrated their success. They had faced countless challenges and overcome them all, their skills and teamwork carrying them through.

Lucas gathered everyone around the table, a rare smile on his face. "We did it. We pulled off the impossible. I'm proud of each and every one of you."

Emma, Jack, and Carl nodded, their faces reflecting a mixture of relief and triumph. They had made history, and they had done it together.

As they divided the spoils and prepared to go their separate ways, Lucas felt a deep sense of satisfaction. They had achieved their goal, and they had done it with precision and unity.

The heist of Fort Knox would go down in history as one of the greatest heists ever pulled off. And it was all thanks to their meticulous planning, unwavering determination, and unbreakable trust in each other.

As the team disbanded, each member heading off to their new lives, Lucas couldn't help but feel a sense of anticipation for the future. They had proven that they were capable of anything, and he knew that whatever challenges lay ahead, they would face them together.

They had made history, and they were ready for whatever came next.

Chapter 7: The Weak Link

The days following the successful blackout mission were filled with cautious optimism. The team felt the adrenaline high of pulling off a near-impossible feat, but Lucas "Lucky" Kane knew better than to let complacency set in. He reminded his team that their biggest challenge was yet to come: the actual heist. As they gathered in the cabin to finalize the plans, an unexpected complication emerged that threatened to unravel everything they had worked for.

Jack "Smooth" Taylor, the con artist, had been riding high on the success of their mission to the power station. His role had been crucial, and his confidence was at an all-time high. But as the team prepared for the heist, Jack's past came back to haunt him in a way that neither he nor the team could have anticipated.

Jack's Past Catches Up With Him

IT WAS A WARM AFTERNOON, and Jack decided to visit a bar he used to frequent in Louisville. He needed a break from the intensity of the planning sessions and wanted to enjoy a drink in a familiar setting. The bar was dimly lit, with the hum of conversations and clinking glasses creating a comforting background noise.

As Jack sat at the bar, nursing his whiskey, he felt a tap on his shoulder. Turning around, he came face to face with a man he hadn't seen in years—Derek "Deke" Simmons, a former partner-in-crime turned bitter rival. Deke was a tall, wiry man with a cunning glint in his eye and a perpetual smirk that suggested he was always one step ahead.

"Jack Taylor," Deke said, his voice dripping with sarcasm. "I never thought I'd see you here again. Still running those cons, I see?"

Jack's heart sank. He knew this encounter could spell trouble. "Deke," he replied coolly, trying to mask his anxiety. "Long time no see. What brings you here?"

Deke leaned in, his smirk widening. "Oh, I heard through the grapevine that you're up to something big. Real big. And I just had to see it for myself."

Jack's mind raced. How could Deke know about the heist? Had someone talked? "I don't know what you're talking about," Jack said, his voice steady despite the turmoil inside.

Deke chuckled. "Come on, Jack. We both know you're not one to play it small. But here's the thing—I want in. Or I might just have to spill the beans to the wrong people."

The Threat

JACK FELT A COLD KNOT form in his stomach. He knew Deke well enough to realize that this wasn't an idle threat. Deke was ruthless and would have no qualms about ruining their plans for his gain. Jack had to think fast.

"Alright, Deke," Jack said, forcing a smile. "Let's not get hasty. How about we discuss this somewhere private?"

Deke nodded, and they moved to a secluded corner of the bar. Jack knew he had to find a way to deal with Deke without jeopardizing the heist. As they sat down, Deke's eyes gleamed with anticipation.

"So, what's the play, Jack?" Deke asked. "I want a piece of the action. And if I don't get it, well, you know what happens next."

Jack took a deep breath, his mind working overtime. "Okay, here's the deal. I can cut you in, but you need to keep your mouth shut. We're talking serious money here, but if you blow this for us, there won't be anything for anyone."

Deke leaned back, considering the offer. "How much are we talking?"

Jack named a figure, hoping it would be enough to satisfy Deke's greed. "It's a huge score, Deke. More than enough for all of us. But you have to promise me you'll stay quiet and let us handle the plan."

Deke seemed to mull it over, his smirk never leaving his face. "Alright, Jack. You've got a deal. But if you try to screw me over, I'll make sure you regret it."

Jack nodded, feeling a temporary sense of relief. But he knew that Deke was a loose cannon, and this was a ticking time bomb that could explode at any moment.

The Desperate Measures

BACK AT THE CABIN, Jack couldn't shake the feeling of dread. He needed to tell Lucas and the team about Deke, but he also knew that it could create panic and distrust. He decided to wait for the right moment, hoping that he could handle the situation on his own.

As the days passed, Jack's anxiety grew. He knew that Deke would demand his share soon, and he needed a plan to silence him without jeopardizing the heist. He spent hours brainstorming and considering his options, but nothing seemed foolproof.

One evening, as the team gathered to review the final details of the heist, Jack's phone buzzed with a message from Deke: "Time's up, Jack. I want my share now."

Jack's heart pounded as he read the message. He knew he couldn't keep this from the team any longer. Taking a deep breath, he addressed Lucas and the others.

"Guys, we have a problem," Jack said, his voice tense. "An old rival of mine, Deke Simmons, found out about our heist. He's threatening to expose us unless he gets a cut."

The room fell silent, the gravity of the situation sinking in. Lucas's eyes narrowed as he processed the information. "How did he find out?" Lucas asked, his voice calm but intense.

"I don't know," Jack admitted. "But he's serious. If we don't deal with him, he'll ruin everything."

Emma and Carl exchanged worried glances, understanding the potential threat this posed. Lucas stood up, his mind racing. "Alright, we need to handle this carefully. Jack, you're the one who knows him best. What do you suggest?"

Jack took a deep breath, knowing that his next words could determine the fate of their entire plan. "I think we need to pay him off, at least for now. But we also need a contingency plan in case he tries to double-cross us."

Lucas nodded. "Alright. We'll set up a meeting and pay him off. But we need to be prepared for any eventuality. Emma, can you set up surveillance to monitor the meeting?"

Emma nodded, her expression determined. "I'll handle it. We'll know if he tries anything."

The Meeting with Deke

THE TEAM SET UP THE meeting with Deke in an abandoned warehouse on the outskirts of town. It was a location they had used before for their dry runs, and it provided the privacy they needed to handle the situation.

Jack arrived early, his nerves on edge. He knew that this meeting could make or break their heist. Lucas, Emma, and Carl were stationed nearby, ready to intervene if things went south.

Deke arrived a few minutes later, his smirk firmly in place. "Jack," he said, his voice dripping with mock friendliness. "Good to see you again."

Jack forced a smile. "Deke. Let's get this over with."

Deke's eyes gleamed with anticipation. "Show me the money."

Jack handed over a briefcase filled with cash, hoping it would be enough to satisfy Deke. "This is your share. Now, keep your mouth shut and let us handle the rest."

Deke opened the briefcase, his eyes widening at the sight of the money. "Well, well, Jack. You've outdone yourself. This should do nicely."

But as Deke closed the briefcase, his smirk turned into a sneer. "You know, Jack, I've been thinking. Maybe I want more. Maybe I want in on the whole thing."

Jack's heart sank. He knew that Deke was pushing his luck, and this could escalate quickly. "Deke, we had a deal. Don't push it."

Deke stepped closer, his expression menacing. "Or what, Jack? You'll take me out? I don't think you have it in you."

At that moment, Lucas's voice came through Jack's earpiece. "Stay calm, Jack. We're ready to move if things get out of hand."

Jack took a deep breath, trying to remain calm. "Deke, don't do this. Take the money and walk away."

But Deke's eyes glinted with greed and malice. "No, Jack. I want in. And if you don't agree, I'll make sure everyone knows about your little plan."

The Desperate Measures

REALIZING THAT NEGOTIATIONS had broken down, Jack knew he had to act. He glanced around, making sure the team was in position. "Alright, Deke. You win. You're in."

Deke's smirk returned, but before he could respond, Carl emerged from the shadows, his imposing figure casting a long shadow. "Time's up, Deke," Carl said, his voice low and menacing.

Deke's eyes widened in surprise and fear. "What the hell is this, Jack?"

Jack stepped back, his expression cold. "This is the end of the line, Deke. You should have taken the deal."

Before Deke could react, Carl moved swiftly, grabbing him by the collar and pinning him against the wall. "We're done playing games," Carl growled. "You're going to disappear, and if you ever come back, it'll be the last thing you do."

Deke struggled, but Carl's grip was unbreakable. "You can't do this!" Deke spat, panic in his eyes.

Jack stepped forward, his voice icy. "We can and we will. You're a loose end, Deke. And loose ends get tied up."

Emma, monitoring the situation from her laptop, spoke through their earpieces. "Everything's clear. No sign of anyone else nearby."

Lucas, watching from a distance, nodded. "Take care of it, Carl."

Carl tightened his grip, his eyes boring into Deke's. "You have two choices, Deke. Leave town and never come back, or we'll make sure you're never a problem again."

Deke's fear turned to desperation. "Alright, alright! I'll leave! Just let me go!"

Carl released him, and Deke stumbled back, clutching the briefcase. "Get out of here," Carl said, his voice like steel. "And remember, we'll be watching."

Deke nodded frantically, backing away before turning and running out of the warehouse. Jack watched him go, a mixture of relief and lingering fear in his eyes.

The Aftermath

WITH DEKE GONE, THE team regrouped at the cabin. The tension was palpable, but there was also a sense of relief. They had dealt with a major threat, but the incident had shaken them.

"Good job handling that, Jack," Lucas said, his expression serious. "But we need to make sure there are no more surprises. We can't afford any more loose ends."

Jack nodded, feeling the weight of his actions. "I'm sorry for bringing this on us. I thought I could handle it."

Lucas placed a reassuring hand on Jack's shoulder. "You did what you had to do. We're a team, and we'll get through this together."

Emma and Carl nodded in agreement, their expressions reflecting a renewed sense of determination. They knew that the heist was still ahead, and they needed to be united and focused.

The team spent the next few days reinforcing their plans, running through simulations, and ensuring that every detail was accounted for. They couldn't afford any more mistakes, and they were determined to pull off the heist flawlessly.

The Final Preparations

AS THE DAY OF THE HEIST approached, the team's nerves were on edge, but their resolve was stronger than ever. They had faced numerous challenges and overcome them all, and now they were ready for the ultimate test.

Lucas gathered the team for one final briefing. "We've planned and prepared for this moment. We know the risks, but we also know our strengths. Trust in your skills and trust in each other. We've got this."

Emma, Jack, and Carl nodded, their confidence unwavering. They knew the stakes were high, but they also knew they had the skills and the plan to pull it off.

The night before the heist, the team gathered around a fire pit outside the cabin. It was a rare moment of relaxation, the tension of the day easing with the warmth of the fire and the camaraderie that had developed over their time together.

"We've come a long way," Lucas said, his voice reflective. "Tomorrow, we make history. Let's make sure we do it right."

Emma smiled, her eyes reflecting the firelight. "We're ready. We've planned for every scenario."

Jack grinned, his usual confidence shining through. "I'm ready for the challenge."

Carl nodded, his expression determined. "Let's do this."

As they sat around the fire, sharing stories and laughter, the bonds of friendship and trust grew stronger. They knew that the heist would be their greatest challenge, but they also knew that they were ready.

The next morning, they would embark on the most ambitious heist of their careers. They had planned meticulously, overcome numerous obstacles, and faced their fears. Now, it was time to put their plan into action and make history.

As the fire died down and the team headed to bed, Lucas felt a sense of calm and confidence. They were ready for whatever came their way. Tomorrow, they would make history.

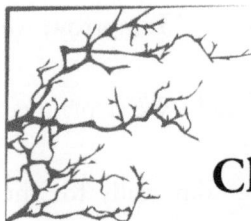

Chapter 8: Tensions Rise

The initial euphoria following their encounter with Deke Simmons had waned, replaced by a tense and uneasy atmosphere within the team. Lucas "Lucky" Kane sensed it immediately. Their meticulously planned heist was teetering on the brink of chaos, not because of external threats but due to the growing mistrust and internal conflicts among his team. As the leader, Lucas knew it was his responsibility to maintain cohesion and resolve these conflicts before they jeopardized everything they had worked for.

Growing Mistrust Within the Team

THE TEAM HAD GATHERED in their secluded cabin, reviewing the final details of their heist. Despite the apparent focus on the task at hand, the undercurrent of suspicion was palpable. Emma Hayes, the tech genius, had started to question Carl "Tank" Johnson's methods. Jack "Smooth" Taylor was still on edge after the encounter with Deke, and his anxiety was spreading to the others. Carl, always the stoic enforcer, had become increasingly impatient with the perceived lack of action.

Lucas could see the tension in their faces. Emma was furiously typing on her laptop, her eyes flicking up every so often to glare at Carl. Jack was pacing, his usual confident swagger replaced by restless energy. Carl sat in a corner, arms crossed, his expression dark and brooding.

"We need to talk," Lucas said, breaking the silence. "There's too much tension in this room. We need to clear the air before we move forward."

Emma stopped typing and looked up, her eyes cold. "I agree. We need to address the elephant in the room. Carl's methods are too brute force for this operation. We need precision, not muscle."

Carl's eyes narrowed. "And what's that supposed to mean? You think your tech can solve everything? Sometimes you need to get your hands dirty."

Jack stopped pacing and turned to face the others. "We all have our roles to play. But we need to trust each other. Right now, it feels like we're falling apart."

Lucas Tries to Maintain Cohesion and Resolve Conflicts

LUCAS KNEW HE HAD TO intervene before things escalated further. "Listen," he said, his voice firm but calm. "We're a team, and we've come too far to let mistrust tear us apart. Emma, your tech skills are crucial to our success. Carl, your strength and tactical knowledge are equally important. We need both."

Emma's expression softened slightly, but her eyes remained wary. "I just want to make sure we're not relying too much on brute force. This heist requires finesse."

Carl uncrossed his arms and leaned forward. "And I want to make sure we're not overcomplicating things. Sometimes the simplest solution is the best one."

Jack nodded, stepping in to mediate. "We need a balance. Emma, you focus on the tech. Carl, you handle the physical security. We all have our strengths, and we need to play to them."

Lucas watched as the tension in the room began to ease. "Good. Now, let's focus on the task at hand. We need to go over the plan one more time and make sure everyone is on the same page."

The team gathered around the table, and Lucas began to outline the final details of their plan. As they worked through the logistics, the atmosphere grew less charged, and the old camaraderie started to return. But Lucas knew that the underlying issues weren't completely resolved. They needed more than just a temporary truce; they needed to rebuild the trust that had been fractured.

Carl's Brute Force Methods Clash with Emma's Tech-Savvy Approach

AS THE TEAM CONTINUED to finalize their plans, the clash between Carl's brute force methods and Emma's tech-savvy approach became more apparent. Emma was focused on the precision and timing required to hack into

Fort Knox's security systems, while Carl believed that physical strength and intimidation were equally important.

During a practice run, Emma was meticulously setting up her equipment, ensuring that every connection was secure and every script was ready to execute. Carl, on the other hand, was growing increasingly impatient.

"Come on, Emma," Carl said, his frustration evident. "We don't have all day. Just get it done."

Emma shot him a withering look. "This isn't something you can rush, Carl. If we make one mistake, the entire operation could be compromised."

Carl's jaw tightened. "And if we get caught because you're too busy playing with your gadgets, it's game over."

Lucas stepped in, sensing the brewing conflict. "Both of you are right. We need precision and speed. Emma, we appreciate your attention to detail, but we also need to move quickly. Carl, give her the time she needs to do her job properly."

Emma sighed, clearly trying to hold her temper. "Fine. Just let me do this my way."

Carl nodded curtly, but Lucas could see that the tension was far from resolved. They needed to find a way to reconcile these two approaches, or risk failure.

A Near-Breach in Their Cover

AS IF THE INTERNAL conflicts weren't enough, the team faced an even greater threat when their cover was nearly blown. Lucas had been meticulous in ensuring that their activities remained undetected, but a minor slip-up nearly led to disaster.

One evening, as they were running through a final practice session, Emma's laptop suddenly pinged with an alert. She frowned and quickly checked her screens. "We have a problem," she said, her voice tense. "Someone's trying to trace our IP address."

Lucas's heart skipped a beat. "How did that happen?"

Emma's fingers flew over the keyboard. "I don't know. But if they trace it back to us, we're finished."

Jack, who had been monitoring the surroundings, rushed over. "What do we do?"

Emma's eyes widened as she continued to type. "I'm setting up a series of decoys to throw them off our trail, but we need to move. Now."

Lucas sprang into action. "Everyone, pack up. We're relocating."

The team moved quickly, gathering their equipment and personal belongings. Emma worked frantically to set up the decoys, her face a mask of concentration. "This should buy us some time, but we need to get out of here."

Carl helped Emma with her equipment, his earlier frustration forgotten. "Let's go. We don't have much time."

Lucas led the team out of the cabin, moving swiftly through the woods to their backup location—a remote safe house they had prepared in case of emergencies. The journey was tense, each member on high alert for any signs of pursuit.

As they reached the safe house and secured the perimeter, Lucas let out a sigh of relief. "Alright, let's get set up again. Emma, keep monitoring the situation and let us know if anything changes."

Emma nodded, already setting up her laptop. "I'll make sure they don't find us."

Rebuilding Trust and Cohesion

THE NEAR-BREACH HAD shaken the team, but it also brought them closer together. As they settled into the safe house, Lucas knew they needed to address the underlying issues once and for all.

"Listen," Lucas said, gathering the team around the table. "We can't afford any more mistakes or conflicts. We need to trust each other completely. Emma, Carl, I need you to find a way to work together."

Emma looked at Carl, her expression softening. "I know we have different approaches, but we both want the same thing. Let's find a way to make this work."

Carl nodded, his demeanor more conciliatory. "Agreed. We need to be a team. Let's figure out how to combine our strengths."

Jack, always the peacemaker, chimed in. "We've faced worse than this and come out on top. We can do it again."

Lucas felt a sense of pride in his team. They had been through a lot, but they were still standing. "Alright. Let's refocus and get back to work. We're almost there."

Final Preparations

WITH THE TENSION EASED and trust beginning to rebuild, the team threw themselves into the final preparations for the heist. They reviewed every detail, ran through simulations, and ensured that their plan was airtight.

Emma fine-tuned her scripts, making sure that everything was ready for the blackout and the infiltration. Carl worked on refining their physical security measures, ensuring that they could handle any obstacles. Jack practiced his role, honing his skills to perfection.

Lucas coordinated their efforts, his mind always on the bigger picture. He knew that they had faced significant challenges, but he also knew that they were capable of pulling off the heist.

The night before the heist, the team gathered for one final meeting. The atmosphere was tense but focused, each member ready to play their part.

"Tomorrow is the day," Lucas said, his voice steady. "We've planned and prepared for this moment. We know the risks, but we also know our strengths. Trust in your skills and trust in each other. We've got this."

Emma, Jack, and Carl nodded, their confidence unwavering. They knew the stakes were high, but they also knew they had the skills and the plan to pull it off.

The Heist Begins

THE MORNING OF THE heist arrived, and the team moved into position. Emma monitored the EMP device, ready to create the blackout. Jack and Carl prepared for their roles, each focused and determined.

Lucas coordinated their movements, ensuring that everything was on track. "Everyone, stay sharp and stick to the plan."

As the countdown timer approached zero, the team held their breath. The EMP device activated, and the blackout began.

"Move!" Lucas ordered, and the team sprang into action.

Emma disabled the security systems, providing real-time updates. "Cameras and alarms are down. You have a clear path."

Jack and Carl moved swiftly, using the cover of darkness to slip past the outer perimeter. They reached the vault, and Emma used the keycard and biometric data to gain access. The vault door opened, revealing the vast reserves of gold inside.

Lucas felt a surge of triumph. They had done it. They had breached Fort Knox.

The Escape

WITH THE GOLD SECURED, the team began their escape. They moved quickly and efficiently, each member playing their role to perfection. Emma monitored the security systems, ensuring they had enough time to get out before the alarms reactivated. Jack and Carl handled any obstacles, their actions smooth and decisive.

Lucas coordinated their movements, keeping everyone on track and focused. "We're almost there. Keep moving."

As they reached the exit, the alarms began to blare. Emma had timed it perfectly, giving them just enough time to escape before the security systems fully reactivated.

The team made their way to their getaway vehicles, the adrenaline pumping through their veins. They had done it. They had pulled off the heist of a lifetime.

The Aftermath

BACK AT THE SAFE HOUSE, the team celebrated their success. They had faced countless challenges and overcome them all, their skills and teamwork carrying them through.

Lucas gathered everyone around the table, a rare smile on his face. "We did it. We pulled off the impossible. I'm proud of each and every one of you."

Emma, Jack, and Carl nodded, their faces reflecting a mixture of relief and triumph. They had made history, and they had done it together.

As they divided the spoils and prepared to go their separate ways, Lucas felt a deep sense of satisfaction. They had achieved their goal, and they had done it with precision and unity.

The heist of Fort Knox would go down in history as one of the greatest heists ever pulled off. And it was all thanks to their meticulous planning, unwavering determination, and unbreakable trust in each other.

As the team disbanded, each member heading off to their new lives, Lucas couldn't help but feel a sense of anticipation for the future. They had proven that they were capable of anything, and he knew that whatever challenges lay ahead, they would face them together.

They had made history, and they were ready for whatever came next.

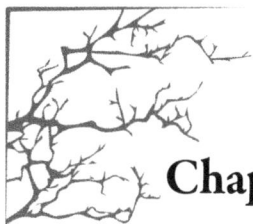

Chapter 9: Final Preparations

T he morning light filtered through the windows of the cabin, casting a warm glow on the faces of Lucas "Lucky" Kane and his team. They had been through intense planning, practice runs, and near-disasters, but now they were on the brink of the most ambitious heist of their lives. The tension was palpable, but Lucas knew that the final preparations were crucial. It was time to address each team member's fears and motivations, ensuring that they were all ready for the challenges ahead.

Addressing Fears and Motivations

LUCAS GATHERED HIS team around the table in the cabin's main room. Emma Hayes, the tech genius, Jack "Smooth" Taylor, the con artist, and Carl "Tank" Johnson, the muscle, all looked at him with a mixture of anticipation and anxiety. They were ready, but Lucas knew that their fears needed to be addressed before they could proceed with confidence.

"Alright, everyone," Lucas began, his voice steady and reassuring. "We've been through a lot together, and now we're almost at the finish line. But before we go any further, I want to address any fears or concerns you might have. We need to be completely open and honest with each other."

Emma was the first to speak up, her eyes betraying the anxiety she had been trying to hide. "I'm worried about the tech failing at the last minute. I've double-checked everything, but there's always a chance something could go wrong."

Lucas nodded, understanding her concerns. "Emma, your skills have been the backbone of this operation. We all trust your expertise. But I also understand the pressure you're under. We've prepared for every contingency, and we have backup plans in place. Trust in your abilities and know that we're all here to support you."

Jack leaned forward, his usual confidence tempered by a rare moment of vulnerability. "I've been thinking about Deke and the possibility that he might still try to interfere. I know we dealt with him, but I can't shake the feeling that he's a ticking time bomb."

Lucas placed a reassuring hand on Jack's shoulder. "We've taken precautions to ensure Deke won't be a problem. But I understand your concern. Keep your focus on the task at hand and trust that we've covered all our bases. We're a team, and we'll handle whatever comes our way together."

Carl, ever the stoic presence, finally spoke up. "My main worry is that we'll encounter something we didn't plan for. I know we've run countless simulations, but there's always that unknown factor."

Lucas looked at Carl, appreciating his honesty. "You're right, Carl. There are always unknowns. But we've trained for this. Your strength and quick thinking are vital to our success. Trust in your instincts and your training. We're ready for whatever comes our way."

With their fears addressed and their motivations reaffirmed, the team felt a renewed sense of unity and purpose. They knew that the heist would be challenging, but they also knew that they were prepared.

Emma Fine-Tunes the Tech Equipment

WITH THE EMOTIONAL groundwork laid, it was time for Emma to focus on fine-tuning the tech equipment. The success of their heist depended heavily on her ability to disable the security systems at Fort Knox and ensure a seamless operation.

Emma set up her workstation in the cabin, surrounded by laptops, wires, and various gadgets. She had already spent countless hours programming and testing her scripts, but now she needed to ensure everything was perfect.

Lucas watched as Emma worked, her fingers flying over the keyboard with practiced precision. "How's it looking, Emma?"

Emma didn't look up from her screen. "I'm running the final diagnostics now. Everything seems to be in order, but I want to make sure there are no last-minute surprises."

Lucas nodded, satisfied with her dedication. "Take all the time you need. We'll be ready when you are."

As Emma continued her work, she couldn't help but feel the weight of responsibility on her shoulders. The team was counting on her, and failure wasn't an option. She double-checked the EMP device, ensuring that it was programmed correctly to create the temporary blackout they needed. She also reviewed the scripts that would disable the security cameras and alarms, making sure they were flawless.

Hours passed, and Emma's concentration never wavered. Finally, she leaned back in her chair, a satisfied smile on her face. "All systems are go. We're ready."

Jack Secures Escape Routes and Backup Plans

WHILE EMMA FOCUSED on the tech, Jack "Smooth" Taylor turned his attention to securing the escape routes and backup plans. His role was to ensure that they had multiple ways out of Fort Knox, regardless of what obstacles they might encounter.

Jack had always been a master of improvisation, but he knew that this heist required meticulous planning. He pulled out a map of the area surrounding Fort Knox and began plotting their escape routes. He identified several key points where they could stash getaway vehicles and mapped out alternate routes in case their primary path was compromised.

Lucas joined Jack, studying the map. "What's the plan, Jack?"

Jack pointed to several locations on the map. "We'll have three main escape routes, each with a backup plan. I've arranged for vehicles to be hidden at these points. If something goes wrong, we can switch to one of the alternates and still make it out clean."

Lucas nodded, impressed by Jack's thoroughness. "Good work. What about contingencies? If we get separated or one of the routes is blocked?"

Jack had already thought of that. "I've set up rendezvous points along each route. If we get separated, we'll regroup at the nearest one. I've also arranged for safe houses in case we need to lay low for a while."

Lucas smiled, feeling a sense of relief. "You've covered everything. Excellent job, Jack."

Jack grinned, his confidence returning. "We've got this, Lucas. We'll be in and out before they even know what hit them."

Carl Tests and Refines the Physical Entry Tactics

WITH THE TECH AND ESCAPE plans in place, it was time for Carl "Tank" Johnson to test and refine their physical entry tactics. Carl's role was to handle any physical obstacles they might encounter and ensure that they could breach the vault with minimal resistance.

Carl had set up a mock version of the Fort Knox vault in the cabin's basement, complete with reinforced doors and simulated security measures. He spent hours practicing his entry techniques, using a combination of brute force and finesse to overcome the various obstacles.

Lucas watched as Carl worked, his powerful frame moving with surprising agility. "How's it going, Carl?"

Carl paused, wiping sweat from his brow. "I've got the entry tactics down. But I want to run through it a few more times to make sure there are no surprises."

Lucas nodded, appreciating Carl's dedication. "Take all the time you need. We need to be perfect."

Carl continued to practice, refining his techniques and ensuring that he could breach the vault quickly and efficiently. He also tested the tools and equipment they would use, making sure everything was in top condition.

As the day turned into night, Carl finally felt satisfied with his preparations. He joined Lucas and the rest of the team, a determined look on his face. "We're ready. Let's do this."

Final Briefing

WITH ALL THE PREPARATIONS complete, Lucas called the team together for a final briefing. The atmosphere was tense but focused, each member ready to play their part in the heist.

"Alright, everyone," Lucas began, his voice steady and confident. "This is it. We've planned and prepared for this moment. We know the risks, but we also know our strengths. Trust in your skills and trust in each other. We've got this."

Emma nodded, her confidence in the tech equipment unwavering. "All systems are go. We're ready to disable the security and create the blackout."

Jack grinned, his usual swagger returning. "I've secured the escape routes and backup plans. We've got multiple ways out, no matter what happens."

Carl's expression was resolute. "The entry tactics are solid. We'll breach the vault quickly and efficiently."

Lucas looked at each member of his team, feeling a sense of pride and determination. "We've faced countless challenges and overcome them all. Now, it's time to make history. Let's do this."

The Night Before the Heist

AS THE FINAL PREPARATIONS were completed, the team gathered for one last night together before the heist. The tension had eased slightly, replaced by a sense of camaraderie and shared purpose.

Lucas had arranged for a simple meal, and the team sat around the table, enjoying a rare moment of relaxation. They laughed and shared stories, the bonds of friendship growing stronger.

Emma raised her glass, her eyes shining with determination. "To us. We've come a long way, and tomorrow we make history."

Jack clinked his glass against hers, his grin infectious. "To the best damn team I've ever had the pleasure of working with."

Carl nodded, his expression serious but warm. "To success and to us."

Lucas smiled, feeling a sense of contentment. "To us. Let's show them what we're made of."

As the night wore on, the team retired to their rooms, each member reflecting on the journey that had brought them to this point. They knew that the heist would be their greatest challenge, but they also knew that they were ready.

The Morning of the Heist

THE MORNING OF THE heist dawned clear and bright. The team gathered at the safe house, their faces reflecting a mixture of anticipation and resolve.

Lucas addressed them one final time. "This is it. We've planned, we've prepared, and now it's time to execute. Trust in your skills and trust in each other. We've got this."

Emma, Jack, and Carl nodded, their confidence unwavering. They knew the stakes were high, but they also knew they had the skills and the plan to pull it off.

The team moved into position, each member focused and ready. Emma monitored the EMP device, ready to create the blackout. Jack and Carl prepared for their roles, each determined to succeed.

Lucas coordinated their movements, ensuring that everything was on track. "Everyone, stay sharp and stick to the plan."

As the countdown timer approached zero, the team held their breath. The EMP device activated, and the blackout began.

"Move!" Lucas ordered, and the team sprang into action.

The Heist Begins

EMMA DISABLED THE SECURITY systems, providing real-time updates. "Cameras and alarms are down. You have a clear path."

Jack and Carl moved swiftly, using the cover of darkness to slip past the outer perimeter. They reached the vault, and Emma used the keycard and biometric data to gain access. The vault door opened, revealing the vast reserves of gold inside.

Lucas felt a surge of triumph. They had done it. They had breached Fort Knox.

With the gold secured, the team began their escape. They moved quickly and efficiently, each member playing their role to perfection. Emma monitored the security systems, ensuring they had enough time to get out before the alarms reactivated. Jack and Carl handled any obstacles, their actions smooth and decisive.

Lucas coordinated their movements, keeping everyone on track and focused. "We're almost there. Keep moving."

As they reached the exit, the alarms began to blare. Emma had timed it perfectly, giving them just enough time to escape before the security systems fully reactivated.

The team made their way to their getaway vehicles, the adrenaline pumping through their veins. They had done it. They had pulled off the heist of a lifetime.

The Aftermath

BACK AT THE SAFE HOUSE, the team celebrated their success. They had faced countless challenges and overcome them all, their skills and teamwork carrying them through.

Lucas gathered everyone around the table, a rare smile on his face. "We did it. We pulled off the impossible. I'm proud of each and every one of you."

Emma, Jack, and Carl nodded, their faces reflecting a mixture of relief and triumph. They had made history, and they had done it together.

As they divided the spoils and prepared to go their separate ways, Lucas felt a deep sense of satisfaction. They had achieved their goal, and they had done it with precision and unity.

The heist of Fort Knox would go down in history as one of the greatest heists ever pulled off. And it was all thanks to their meticulous planning, unwavering determination, and unbreakable trust in each other.

As the team disbanded, each member heading off to their new lives, Lucas couldn't help but feel a sense of anticipation for the future. They had proven that they were capable of anything, and he knew that whatever challenges lay ahead, they would face them together.

They had made history, and they were ready for whatever came next.

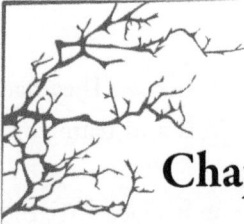

Chapter 10: The Heist Begins

The day of the heist arrived with an air of anticipation so thick it was almost palpable. Lucas "Lucky" Kane and his team had spent months planning and preparing for this moment, and now they stood on the brink of making history. The morning sun cast long shadows across their safe house, a secluded cabin in the woods that had served as their headquarters. Inside, the team was focused and ready, each member going over their role one final time.

Lucas gathered Emma Hayes, the tech genius; Jack "Smooth" Taylor, the con artist; and Carl "Tank" Johnson, the muscle, around the table for a final briefing. This was it—the culmination of all their efforts. The day they would breach the impenetrable fortress of Fort Knox.

"Alright, everyone," Lucas began, his voice steady and reassuring. "This is it. We've planned for every scenario, rehearsed every detail. Now, it's time to execute. Remember, precision and unity. Trust in your skills and trust in each other. Let's make history."

Emma, Jack, and Carl nodded, their confidence unwavering. Each had their own fears and doubts, but they had pushed them aside, focusing solely on the task at hand. They knew the stakes were high, but they also knew they had the skills and the plan to pull it off.

Entering the Premises

THE TEAM MOVED INTO position under the cover of darkness, driving to a remote location near Fort Knox in a nondescript van loaded with their equipment. As they approached the outer perimeter, Emma set up her mobile command center in the back of the van, her laptop and gadgets spread out before her.

"Emma, are you ready?" Lucas asked, his eyes scanning the surroundings.

Emma nodded, her fingers flying over the keyboard. "I'm in position. Disabling the outer perimeter cameras now."

The team watched as Emma's screen showed the feeds from the security cameras around Fort Knox. One by one, the cameras went dark as Emma executed her scripts, creating a temporary blind spot for their approach.

"Cameras are down," Emma reported. "We have a ten-minute window before the system resets."

Lucas turned to Jack and Carl. "Let's move."

Jack and Carl exited the van, moving swiftly and silently towards the fence. Jack, ever the smooth operator, pulled out a set of lock-picking tools and began working on the gate. Within moments, the lock clicked open, and Carl pushed the gate aside, allowing them to slip inside.

"Gate is open," Jack whispered into his earpiece. "Moving to the next checkpoint."

As they advanced, Emma monitored their progress, keeping an eye on the security systems. "You're clear to proceed. Motion sensors are offline."

Jack and Carl moved through the shadows, using the cover of darkness to their advantage. They reached the first security checkpoint, where a guard was patrolling. Jack nodded to Carl, who moved swiftly and silently, subduing the guard with a chokehold and dragging him into the bushes.

"Checkpoint secured," Carl reported. "Moving to the next phase."

Neutralizing Initial Security

THE TEAM CONTINUED their advance, reaching the entrance to the main building. Here, they encountered the first major obstacle: a biometric lock that required both a retinal scan and a fingerprint.

"Emma, we're at the entrance," Jack said, his voice tense. "Ready for the biometric bypass."

Emma's hands flew over the keyboard as she accessed the building's security system. "I'm sending the override codes now. Hold the scanner in place."

Jack positioned the portable scanner over the lock, and within moments, the lock clicked open. "We're in," he whispered. "Moving inside."

Inside the building, the team faced a labyrinth of hallways and security measures. Emma guided them through the maze, disabling cameras and sensors as they went. They reached the main security hub, where they needed to gain control of the entire system.

"Emma, we're at the security hub," Lucas said. "Can you get us inside?"

Emma nodded, her focus intense. "I'm working on it. Give me a minute."

As Emma hacked into the security hub, Jack and Carl kept watch, ready to deal with any guards or obstacles. The seconds ticked by, each one feeling like an eternity. Finally, Emma's voice came through their earpieces.

"I'm in. You should be able to access the security panel now."

Lucas entered the security hub, quickly accessing the panel and disabling the remaining security measures. "We have control of the system. Moving to the vault."

Unforeseen Complications

THE TEAM MOVED SWIFTLY towards the vault, their progress smooth and efficient. But as they reached the final corridor, an unforeseen complication arose. The alarms suddenly blared, and red lights flashed along the hallway.

"Emma, what's going on?" Lucas asked, his heart racing.

Emma's fingers flew over the keyboard. "I'm not sure. It looks like a secondary security protocol was triggered. I'm trying to shut it down."

As Emma worked to disable the alarms, the team took cover, preparing for the worst. The sound of approaching footsteps echoed through the corridor, and Lucas knew they had to act fast.

"Jack, Carl, get ready," Lucas said. "We have company."

A group of guards rounded the corner, their weapons drawn. Jack stepped forward, his usual charm replaced by steely determination. "Leave this to me."

Jack moved with surprising speed, disarming the first guard and using him as a shield. Carl joined the fray, his brute strength overpowering the remaining guards. Within moments, the guards were subdued, but Lucas knew they didn't have much time.

"Emma, we need those alarms off now," Lucas urged.

"I'm almost there," Emma replied, her voice tense. "Just a few more seconds."

The alarms suddenly ceased, and the red lights stopped flashing. Emma's voice came through their earpieces, filled with relief. "Alarms are down. You're clear to proceed."

Lucas nodded, his heart still pounding. "Good work, everyone. Let's move."

Agent Tom Harris's Role

AS THEY APPROACHED the vault, Agent Tom Harris's role became critical. Tom had been blackmailed into aiding the team, and his insider knowledge was crucial to their success. Lucas contacted Tom through a secure channel, ensuring that everything was in place.

"Tom, we're at the vault. Are you ready?" Lucas asked.

Tom's voice came through, calm but tense. "I'm ready. I've disabled the internal security measures and set the biometric scanners to accept your data. You should be able to access the vault."

"Thanks, Tom. We couldn't have done this without you," Lucas replied.

Tom's voice softened slightly. "Just make sure you keep your end of the deal. I've put everything on the line for this."

Lucas nodded, even though Tom couldn't see him. "We will. Just stay focused."

With Tom's assistance, the team approached the vault door. Emma used the keycard and biometric data to bypass the final security measures, and the massive door slowly began to open. Inside, they saw the vast reserves of gold they had been aiming for.

"We're in," Lucas said, a sense of triumph in his voice. "Let's get to work."

Retrieving the Gold

THE TEAM MOVED QUICKLY, loading the gold into specially designed cases that were easy to transport. Each case was equipped with a GPS jammer to prevent tracking, and they worked with military precision, each member knowing their role.

"Keep an eye on the time," Lucas reminded them. "We need to be out of here before the backup systems kick in."

As they worked, Lucas couldn't help but feel a sense of pride in his team. They had faced numerous challenges and overcome them all. Now, they were on the verge of pulling off one of the greatest heists in history.

The Escape

WITH THE GOLD SECURED, the team began their escape. Emma monitored the security systems, ensuring they had enough time to get out before the alarms reactivated. Jack and Carl handled any remaining obstacles, their actions smooth and decisive.

As they reached the exit, the alarms began to blare again, signaling that the backup systems were coming online. Emma had timed it perfectly, giving them just enough time to escape before the security systems fully reactivated.

The team made their way to their getaway vehicles, the adrenaline pumping through their veins. They had done it. They had pulled off the heist of a lifetime.

The Aftermath

BACK AT THE SAFE HOUSE, the team celebrated their success. They had faced countless challenges and overcome them all, their skills and teamwork carrying them through.

Lucas gathered everyone around the table, a rare smile on his face. "We did it. We pulled off the impossible. I'm proud of each and every one of you."

Emma, Jack, and Carl nodded, their faces reflecting a mixture of relief and triumph. They had made history, and they had done it together.

As they divided the spoils and prepared to go their separate ways, Lucas felt a deep sense of satisfaction. They had achieved their goal, and they had done it with precision and unity.

The heist of Fort Knox would go down in history as one of the greatest heists ever pulled off. And it was all thanks to their meticulous planning, unwavering determination, and unbreakable trust in each other.

As the team disbanded, each member heading off to their new lives, Lucas couldn't help but feel a sense of anticipation for the future. They had proven that they were capable of anything, and he knew that whatever challenges lay ahead, they would face them together.

They had made history, and they were ready for whatever came next.

Chapter 11: In the Vault

The adrenaline was palpable as Lucas "Lucky" Kane and his team stood before the massive vault door of Fort Knox. They had come this far through meticulous planning, precise execution, and sheer determination. But now, as they reached the heart of the fortress, they were about to face their greatest challenge yet.

"Alright, everyone," Lucas said, his voice steady despite the tension. "This is it. Emma, you're up."

Emma Hayes, the tech genius of the team, stepped forward with her equipment. She had already bypassed numerous security systems to get them this far, but the vault door presented a new level of complexity.

"Give me a minute," Emma said, her fingers flying over her keyboard. "I need to sync the biometric data and override the final lock."

As Emma worked, Jack "Smooth" Taylor and Carl "Tank" Johnson kept a vigilant watch. The sense of urgency was heightened by the knowledge that they were deep inside one of the most secure facilities in the world, with only minutes to complete their mission.

Surprise Security Upgrade

JUST AS EMMA WAS ABOUT to complete the override, her screen flashed with an unexpected alert. "Damn it!" she muttered, her face paling. "They've upgraded the security protocols. This wasn't in the plans."

Lucas stepped closer, his eyes narrowing. "What do you mean, upgraded?"

Emma pointed to the screen, which displayed a series of complex security algorithms. "They've added a new layer of encryption and a secondary biometric scan. It's going to take more time to bypass."

Jack cursed under his breath. "We don't have more time. The guards will be on us any minute."

Lucas clenched his jaw. "Emma, do whatever it takes. Carl and I will handle the guards. Jack, stay with Emma and keep an eye on the hallway."

Emma nodded, her fingers flying over the keyboard faster than ever. "I'm on it. Just keep them off me for a few more minutes."

Fending Off Guards

AS EMMA WORKED AGAINST the clock, Lucas and Carl positioned themselves near the entrance to the vault corridor. The sound of approaching footsteps echoed through the hallway, signaling the arrival of the guards.

Carl, ever the enforcer, flexed his massive arms. "Here they come. Let's make sure they don't get past us."

Lucas nodded, drawing his weapon. "We hold this line. No matter what."

The first guards rounded the corner, their eyes widening in surprise at the sight of the intruders. Lucas fired a warning shot, causing them to take cover.

"Stay back!" Lucas shouted, his voice echoing through the corridor.

Carl moved with surprising speed, engaging the guards in close combat. His strength and skill were unmatched, and within moments, he had disarmed and incapacitated two of them. But more were coming, and the sound of the alarm blaring in the background added to the urgency.

"We've got more company!" Carl called out, his voice strained but determined.

Lucas fired at the advancing guards, buying Emma precious seconds to complete her task. "Emma, how's it going?"

"I'm almost there!" Emma replied, her voice tense. "Just a little more time."

Bypassing the New Security Protocols

EMMA'S FINGERS FLEW over the keyboard, her mind racing to decipher the new encryption and bypass the secondary biometric scan. She knew that failure was not an option, and the pressure was immense.

"Come on, come on," she muttered, her eyes focused on the screen. She typed in a series of commands, hoping to find a backdoor into the system.

Behind her, Jack kept a vigilant watch, ready to spring into action if needed. "You're doing great, Emma. Just keep going."

Emma's heart pounded as she worked. She managed to break through the first layer of encryption, but the secondary biometric scan proved to be more challenging. She had to create a false scan that would fool the system, and time was running out.

Finally, with a triumphant beep, the screen flashed green. "I'm in!" Emma exclaimed, her voice filled with relief. "The vault is unlocked."

Gaining Access to the Treasure

LUCAS AND CARL HELD their ground, fending off the guards with relentless determination. As Emma's voice came through their earpieces, a sense of triumph surged through them.

"Great job, Emma," Lucas said, his voice steady despite the chaos. "Jack, get that door open."

Jack moved quickly, entering the final command to unlock the vault door. The massive door slowly swung open, revealing the vast reserves of gold inside.

"We're in," Jack said, his voice filled with awe. "Let's get to work."

The team moved swiftly, loading the gold into specially designed cases. Each case was equipped with a GPS jammer to prevent tracking, and they worked with military precision, each member knowing their role.

"Keep an eye on the time," Lucas reminded them. "We need to be out of here before the backup systems kick in."

As they worked, the sound of approaching guards grew louder. Carl and Lucas continued to hold them off, buying Emma and Jack the time they needed to secure the treasure.

"We've got about five minutes before the alarms reset," Emma warned, her voice urgent. "We need to move."

Lucas nodded, his mind racing with the logistics of their escape. "Alright, let's wrap it up. Carl, help me secure the last cases."

Final Moments in the Vault

THE TEAM WORKED WITH precision and efficiency, their movements coordinated and deliberate. As they loaded the final case, Lucas felt a surge of triumph. They had done it—they had breached the vault of Fort Knox.

But their success was tempered by the knowledge that they still had to escape. The guards were relentless, and the backup security systems were about to come online.

"Time's up," Emma said, her voice steady despite the tension. "We need to go. Now."

Lucas gave a final nod, his eyes scanning the vault one last time. "Let's move. Everyone, stick to the plan."

The Escape

THE TEAM MOVED QUICKLY, each member playing their role to perfection. Emma monitored the security systems, ensuring they had enough time to get out before the alarms reactivated. Jack and Carl handled any remaining obstacles, their actions smooth and decisive.

As they reached the exit, the alarms began to blare again, signaling that the backup systems were coming online. Emma had timed it perfectly, giving them just enough time to escape before the security systems fully reactivated.

The team made their way to their getaway vehicles, the adrenaline pumping through their veins. They had done it. They had pulled off the heist of a lifetime.

The Aftermath

BACK AT THE SAFE HOUSE, the team celebrated their success. They had faced countless challenges and overcome them all, their skills and teamwork carrying them through.

Lucas gathered everyone around the table, a rare smile on his face. "We did it. We pulled off the impossible. I'm proud of each and every one of you."

Emma, Jack, and Carl nodded, their faces reflecting a mixture of relief and triumph. They had made history, and they had done it together.

As they divided the spoils and prepared to go their separate ways, Lucas felt a deep sense of satisfaction. They had achieved their goal, and they had done it with precision and unity.

The heist of Fort Knox would go down in history as one of the greatest heists ever pulled off. And it was all thanks to their meticulous planning, unwavering determination, and unbreakable trust in each other.

Reflections and Future Plans

AS THE CELEBRATION continued, Lucas found a quiet moment to reflect on the journey that had brought them to this point. They had faced numerous challenges and obstacles, but their determination and teamwork had carried them through.

Emma approached him, a thoughtful look on her face. "Lucas, I've been thinking. We've proven that we're capable of pulling off something incredible. What's next for us?"

Lucas smiled, appreciating her forward-thinking attitude. "We'll take some time to enjoy our success and lay low for a while. But after that, who knows? There are always new challenges and opportunities out there. And as long as we stick together, I'm confident we can handle anything."

Jack and Carl joined them, their expressions reflecting a mixture of relief and excitement. "I agree," Jack said. "We've made history, but this is just the beginning. There's so much more we can accomplish."

Carl nodded, his usual stoic demeanor softened by a rare smile. "We've proven that we're a force to be reckoned with. Whatever comes next, I'm ready."

Lucas looked at his team, feeling a deep sense of pride and camaraderie. They had achieved something truly remarkable, and he knew that their bond was unbreakable.

"To the future," Lucas said, raising his glass in a toast. "And to us."

As they clinked their glasses and celebrated their success, Lucas couldn't help but feel a sense of anticipation for what lay ahead. They had made history, and they were ready for whatever challenges and adventures the future might bring.

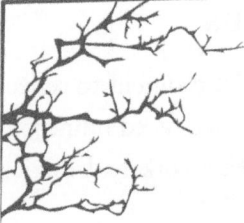

Chapter 12: Betrayal

The exhilaration of successfully breaching the Fort Knox vault was palpable as Lucas "Lucky" Kane and his team made their way through the darkened corridors. The weight of the gold in their specially designed cases was heavy, but their spirits were light. They had done the impossible and were on the brink of escaping with their fortune. However, the euphoria was short-lived as a hidden threat loomed, ready to upend their meticulously crafted plan.

The Double-Cross

THE TEAM HAD NEARLY reached the exit when Lucas's secure comm link buzzed to life. It was Agent Tom Harris, the insider whose critical assistance had been pivotal to their plan. His voice, however, carried an edge of tension that set Lucas on high alert.

"Lucas, we have a problem," Tom said, his voice low and urgent. "Meet me at the southwest exit. Now."

Lucas exchanged a quick glance with Emma, Jack, and Carl. "Stay sharp," he said, signaling for them to follow. "Something's off."

As they approached the designated exit, Lucas saw Tom standing in the shadows, a gun in his hand. The glint in his eye was not one of a man merely concerned about their escape—it was something far more sinister.

"Tom, what's going on?" Lucas asked, his voice steady but his grip tightening on his own weapon.

Tom stepped forward, the tension in the air palpable. "I'm afraid our deal has changed, Lucas. I've been offered a better one."

Before Lucas could respond, a group of armed men emerged from the shadows, their guns trained on the team. It was a setup. Tom had betrayed them.

The Hidden Agenda

"WHO THE HELL ARE THESE guys, Tom?" Carl growled, his massive frame tensing for a fight.

Tom smirked, his eyes cold. "Insurance. You see, Lucas, while your plan was impressive, there are others who would pay much more for the information I possess. This gold is just the icing on the cake."

Lucas's mind raced, trying to piece together the betrayal. "You were never planning to let us walk out of here, were you?"

Tom shrugged. "Let's just say I like to keep my options open. Now, drop your weapons and hand over the gold. Maybe I'll let you live."

Jack's face twisted with anger. "You bastard. We trusted you."

Tom's smirk widened. "Trust is a dangerous thing, Jack. Now, do as I say."

The Deadly Confrontation

THE TENSION REACHED a breaking point as Lucas assessed their options. Surrendering was not one of them. He glanced at Carl, who gave a barely perceptible nod. They would fight.

In a split second, chaos erupted. Lucas dove for cover, firing at Tom's men. Carl charged forward, using his brute strength to overpower two of the armed men before they could react. Emma and Jack took defensive positions, their weapons blazing as they engaged the enemy.

Tom's men were well-trained, but they were not prepared for the ferocity of Lucas's team. Bullets flew, and the air was filled with the deafening roar of gunfire. The confined space made the confrontation even more intense, with every corner and shadow becoming a potential threat.

Emma's tech-savvy instincts kicked in as she hacked into the building's security systems, creating distractions and confusion among Tom's men. "I've disabled their comms," she shouted over the gunfire. "They're blind."

Jack's quick thinking and smooth moves allowed him to flank the enemy, taking out two more men with precision shots. "We need to take out Tom," he yelled. "He's the linchpin."

Lucas knew Jack was right. He focused his efforts on reaching Tom, who had taken cover behind a metal crate. As Lucas moved closer, Tom fired wildly, desperation creeping into his expression.

"Give it up, Tom," Lucas called out. "You can't win this."

Tom's response was a burst of gunfire that missed Lucas by inches. "I'll never surrender," he snarled. "This is my payday."

Unexpected Casualties

IN THE MIDST OF THE chaos, a stray bullet struck Emma's shoulder, sending her crashing to the ground with a cry of pain. "Emma!" Jack shouted, his voice filled with panic.

Carl, seeing Emma go down, unleashed a fury unlike anything the team had ever seen. He charged through the remaining enemies, taking them out with brutal efficiency. But in his rage, he failed to notice one of Tom's men taking aim at him from behind.

A shot rang out, and Carl staggered, clutching his side. Lucas's heart sank as he saw his friend go down, but he couldn't afford to lose focus. With a final surge of determination, he reached Tom's position.

Tom, realizing he was cornered, made a desperate move to flee. Lucas lunged, tackling him to the ground. The two men struggled, their fists flying as they fought for control of the gun. Tom managed to break free, raising his weapon to fire, but Lucas was faster. He disarmed Tom and delivered a knockout blow, leaving the traitor unconscious on the floor.

Critical Decisions

WITH TOM SUBDUED, LUCAS turned his attention to his injured teammates. Emma was pale and bleeding, but conscious. Carl's condition was more serious; he was losing blood fast.

"We need to get out of here," Lucas said, urgency in his voice. "Jack, help me with Carl. Emma, can you walk?"

Emma nodded weakly. "I'll manage. Just get us out of here."

As they made their way to the exit, Lucas knew they were running out of time. The alarms had been triggered during the firefight, and it was only a matter of minutes before reinforcements arrived.

"Jack, you lead the way," Lucas instructed. "Emma, stay close. Carl, hang in there."

They moved as quickly as they could, but the weight of the gold and the injuries slowed them down. Lucas's mind raced, trying to devise a plan to ensure their survival and success.

Ensuring Survival and Success

AS THEY REACHED THE outer perimeter, Lucas spotted a security vehicle parked nearby. It was their best chance for a quick escape. "Jack, get that vehicle started. Emma, help Carl into the back."

Jack sprinted to the vehicle, hotwiring it with practiced ease. Within moments, the engine roared to life. Lucas and Emma helped Carl into the back, securing him as best they could.

"Go, go, go!" Lucas shouted as he climbed into the passenger seat. Jack floored the accelerator, and they sped away from the scene, the alarms fading into the distance.

As they drove, Lucas did a quick assessment of their situation. Emma's shoulder wound needed attention, and Carl's condition was critical. They needed medical help, but going to a hospital was out of the question.

"I know a place," Lucas said, giving Jack directions to a safe house they had prepared for emergencies. "It's not far. We can patch up Carl and regroup."

The drive was tense, each member of the team on high alert for any signs of pursuit. They reached the safe house without incident, and Lucas immediately set to work treating Emma and Carl's injuries.

The Safe House

THE SAFE HOUSE WAS a small, secluded cabin equipped with medical supplies and basic amenities. Lucas laid Carl on a makeshift bed and began treating his wound. Emma, despite her own pain, assisted with the medical supplies.

"You're going to be okay, Carl," Lucas said, his voice firm but gentle. "Just hang in there."

Carl's eyes fluttered open, his face pale but determined. "I'm not checking out yet, boss."

Emma winced as she cleaned her shoulder wound. "We need to talk about what happened back there. Tom's betrayal—how did we not see it coming?"

Lucas shook his head, frustration evident in his expression. "I should have seen the signs. I knew he was under pressure, but I didn't think he'd turn on us."

Jack, who had been keeping watch at the window, turned to face them. "We can't dwell on it now. We need to focus on getting out of this mess and figuring out our next move."

Regrouping and Planning

WITH CARL STABILIZED and Emma's wound treated, the team gathered around the table to regroup. The betrayal had shaken them, but they were far from defeated.

"We need to assess our situation," Lucas said, his tone serious. "We've got the gold, but we need to lay low until things cool down. Tom's betrayal means we have to be extra cautious. There could be more out there who know about us."

Emma nodded, her eyes sharp despite the pain. "We need to check our communications and make sure there are no leaks. I'll handle that."

Jack added, "We also need to plan our exit strategy. We can't stay here forever."

Lucas agreed. "Right. We'll divide the tasks. Emma, secure our comms. Jack, scout the area and make sure we're not being followed. I'll handle the logistics and make contact with our buyer."

As they set to work, the sense of purpose and unity returned. They had faced betrayal and survived, and now they were ready to finish what they had started.

Final Steps

OVER THE NEXT FEW DAYS, the team worked tirelessly to secure their position and plan their next move. Emma ensured their communications were secure, using her tech skills to sweep for any potential breaches. Jack scouted the area, confirming that they were not being pursued. Lucas made contact with their buyer, arranging for a discreet exchange.

Despite the tension and the constant threat of discovery, the team remained focused. They knew that their success depended on their ability to stay united and vigilant.

As the day of the exchange approached, Lucas gathered the team for a final briefing. "We've come this far, and we're not backing down now. The exchange is set for tomorrow. We'll be in and out, no complications."

Emma, Jack, and Carl nodded, their determination unwavering. They knew the risks, but they also knew they had the skills and the plan to pull it off.

The Exchange

THE LOCATION FOR THE exchange was a remote warehouse, chosen for its seclusion and security. The team arrived early, setting up their equipment and securing the perimeter.

Lucas and Jack handled the negotiations, while Emma and Carl kept watch. The buyer, a wealthy and discreet individual, arrived with a small entourage, and the exchange began.

The tension was high as Lucas and the buyer discussed the terms. The gold was inspected, and the payment was confirmed. Everything was going smoothly until one of the buyer's men made a sudden move, drawing a weapon.

A standoff ensued, but Lucas's quick thinking and Jack's smooth talking defused the situation. The buyer, realizing the professionalism and resolve of Lucas's team, ordered his men to stand down.

The exchange was completed, and the team walked away with their payment, their mission accomplished.

Reflection and New Beginnings

BACK AT THE SAFE HOUSE, the team celebrated their success. They had faced betrayal, survived a deadly confrontation, and completed the heist of a lifetime.

Lucas looked at his team, feeling a deep sense of pride and satisfaction. They had proven their resilience and their loyalty to each other.

"We did it," Lucas said, raising a glass. "To us, and to new beginnings."

Emma, Jack, and Carl raised their glasses, their faces reflecting a mixture of relief and triumph. They had made history, and they had done it together.

As they prepared to go their separate ways, Lucas couldn't help but feel a sense of anticipation for the future. They had proven that they were capable of anything, and he knew that whatever challenges lay ahead, they would face them together.

They had made history, and they were ready for whatever came next.

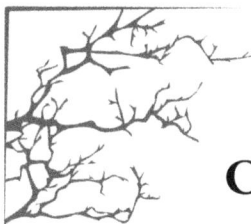

Chapter 13: The Escape

The team's victory at Fort Knox was still fresh in their minds as they gathered their things and prepared to make their final escape. Lucas "Lucky" Kane knew that the hardest part was still ahead. The heist had been a success, but now they faced a high-stakes chase with law enforcement closing in. The sound of distant sirens echoed through the early morning air, a grim reminder that their triumph was far from secure.

The High-Stakes Chase

AS THEY LOADED THE gold into their vehicles, Lucas issued rapid-fire commands to his team. "Emma, Jack, Carl—stick to the plan. We have multiple escape routes, and we'll need to use them to our advantage. Let's get moving."

Emma Hayes, the tech genius, quickly double-checked her equipment, ensuring that their GPS jammers and other electronic countermeasures were active. Jack "Smooth" Taylor, the con artist, was already in the driver's seat of the first getaway car, his mind focused on the elaborate escape plan he had devised. Carl "Tank" Johnson, the muscle, climbed into the second vehicle, ready to handle any physical obstacles they might encounter.

As the team sped away from their safe house, the sound of sirens grew louder. It was clear that law enforcement was closing in, and the tension in the air was palpable.

"We're going to have company soon," Jack said, his voice steady but urgent. "Everyone, stay sharp."

Jack's Elaborate Escape Plan

JACK'S ESCAPE PLAN was nothing short of genius, a complex series of maneuvers designed to throw off any pursuit and ensure the team's safe getaway.

The plan involved splitting up, using decoy vehicles, and exploiting every advantage they had.

"Remember the plan," Lucas reminded them over the comms. "Jack, you take the lead. Emma and Carl, follow his instructions to the letter."

Jack nodded, his eyes focused on the road ahead. "Got it. First, we head to the industrial district. There's a maze of warehouses and side streets that will give us plenty of cover."

The team followed Jack's lead, weaving through the streets of the city. As they reached the industrial district, the sirens grew even closer, the flashing lights of police cars visible in the distance.

Near Captures and Narrow Escapes

THE FIRST REAL TEST of Jack's plan came as they entered the maze of warehouses. The narrow streets and tight corners provided ample opportunities for evasion, but it also meant that any mistake could be costly.

"Take the next left," Jack instructed. "There's an alley that leads to a dead end, but there's a hidden exit behind one of the warehouses."

Emma and Carl followed closely, their vehicles moving in perfect synchronization. As they turned into the alley, they saw the police cars closing in from behind.

"Keep going," Jack urged. "We're almost there."

The alley seemed to lead to a dead end, but Jack's knowledge of the area paid off. He swerved sharply, crashing through a hidden gate that led to a narrow passageway between two buildings. Emma and Carl followed, narrowly avoiding the pursuing police cars.

"Nice move, Jack," Carl said, his voice filled with admiration. "What's next?"

Jack grinned, his confidence growing. "We keep them guessing. There's a series of tunnels beneath the city. We can lose them there."

The team navigated the narrow passageways and emerged onto a main road, blending in with the morning traffic. But the police were relentless, their sirens wailing as they continued the pursuit.

"We need to split up," Lucas said over the comms. "It's the only way to throw them off."

The Team Splits Up

JACK HAD ANTICIPATED this moment and had already planned for it. "Carl, you take the first exit and head towards the docks. Emma, you go east and find a place to lay low. Lucas and I will head to the tunnels."

The team split up, each vehicle taking a different route. Carl sped towards the docks, his powerful frame and determined expression ready for whatever came next. Emma headed east, using her tech skills to find a safe place to hide and monitor the situation.

Lucas and Jack continued towards the tunnels, their car weaving through the traffic with precision. "Stay focused," Lucas said, his voice calm. "We're almost there."

As they reached the entrance to the tunnels, Jack took a sharp turn, entering the dark passageway. The sound of the sirens faded as they descended into the underground maze.

"We've got a bit of breathing room," Jack said, his voice echoing in the tunnel. "But we need to keep moving."

The Underground Maze

THE TUNNELS BENEATH the city were a labyrinth of old sewer systems and maintenance passages. Jack's plan relied on his intimate knowledge of these tunnels, using them to evade the authorities and reach a safe exit point.

"Stick close," Jack instructed. "These tunnels can be confusing if you don't know the way."

Lucas followed Jack's lead, his eyes scanning the dark passageways for any signs of danger. The tunnels were damp and dimly lit, the sound of dripping water echoing around them.

"We're almost at the first checkpoint," Jack said. "There's a hidden exit that leads to an abandoned warehouse. We can regroup there."

As they navigated the tunnels, Lucas couldn't help but admire Jack's resourcefulness. The plan was working, but they couldn't afford to let their guard down.

Carl's Escape to the Docks

MEANWHILE, CARL WAS speeding towards the docks, his mind focused on the task at hand. He knew the area well and had planned several routes to evade any pursuit.

The docks were a maze of shipping containers and warehouses, providing plenty of hiding spots. Carl drove into the heart of the area, using his knowledge of the terrain to stay one step ahead of the police.

As he navigated the narrow passageways between the containers, he spotted a police car in the distance. He quickly turned into a hidden alley, using the shadows to his advantage.

"Just a little further," Carl muttered to himself, his determination unwavering.

He reached a secluded spot and parked the car, blending in with the surrounding containers. He knew he couldn't stay there for long, but it gave him a chance to catch his breath and plan his next move.

Emma's Tech Savvy Evades Pursuit

EMMA, ON THE OTHER hand, was using her tech skills to evade the authorities. She had hacked into the city's traffic cameras and police scanners, giving her real-time updates on their movements.

As she drove east, she monitored the police frequencies, listening for any clues about their pursuit. "They're spreading out," Emma said to herself. "I need to find a place to lay low."

She spotted an old factory building and decided to use it as a temporary hideout. Parking the car inside, she quickly set up her equipment, creating a secure network to monitor the situation.

Emma knew that staying hidden was crucial, but she also needed to keep an eye on her team. She sent a quick message to Lucas and Jack, updating them on her status and offering any assistance they might need.

Lucas and Jack's Narrow Escape

BACK IN THE TUNNELS, Lucas and Jack continued to navigate the underground maze. They reached the first checkpoint, a hidden exit that led to an abandoned warehouse.

Jack pulled the car into the warehouse and parked it behind some old machinery. "We've got a bit of breathing room," he said, his voice filled with relief.

Lucas nodded, his mind already working on their next move. "We need to contact Emma and Carl, make sure they're safe."

Jack quickly set up a secure comm link, reaching out to Emma and Carl. "We're at the warehouse. How's everyone holding up?"

Emma's voice came through the comms, steady and focused. "I'm good. Found a place to lay low and monitoring the situation."

Carl's response was equally reassuring. "I'm at the docks, staying out of sight. What's the next move?"

Lucas took a deep breath, feeling a sense of relief that his team was safe. "We need to regroup and plan our final escape. Let's meet at the secondary safe house in two hours. Stay hidden until then."

The team acknowledged the plan, each member focused on their next move. They knew the authorities would be relentless, but they also knew they had the skills and determination to evade capture.

The Final Stretch

AS THE TEAM PREPARED for the final stretch of their escape, Lucas and Jack took a moment to reflect on the events that had brought them to this point. They had faced countless challenges and overcome them all, but now they were in the final stretch of their journey.

"We've come this far," Lucas said, his voice filled with determination. "We're not backing down now."

Jack nodded, his confidence unwavering. "We've got this, Lucas. Just a little further."

The Secondary Safe House

THE SECONDARY SAFE house was located in a remote area outside the city, a secluded cabin that provided the perfect hideout. The team had prepared it in advance, stocking it with supplies and equipment for their final escape.

As Lucas and Jack approached the safe house, they spotted Emma's car parked outside. "Looks like Emma made it," Jack said, his voice filled with relief.

Inside the cabin, Emma was already set up with her equipment, monitoring the situation and ensuring their communications were secure. "Welcome to the safe house," she said, her eyes reflecting a mixture of relief and determination.

Carl arrived shortly after, his powerful frame filling the doorway as he entered the cabin. "Glad to see everyone made it," he said, his voice steady.

Regrouping and Planning

WITH THE TEAM REUNITED, Lucas gathered them around the table for a final briefing. The escape had been intense, but they had managed to evade capture and reach the safe house.

"We're almost there," Lucas said, his voice filled with determination. "We've faced countless challenges and overcome them all. Now, we just need to finalize our escape and disappear."

Emma, Jack, and Carl nodded, their confidence unwavering. They knew the stakes were high, but they also knew they had the skills and the plan to pull it off.

Finalizing the Escape

THE FINAL ESCAPE PLAN involved splitting up and using different routes to ensure that no one could track them. Each member of the team had a specific role to play, and they knew that their success depended on their ability to stay united and vigilant.

"Emma, you'll head north and use your tech skills to monitor the situation," Lucas instructed. "Jack, you go west and use your connections to secure safe passage. Carl, you head south and use your strength to handle any obstacles."

Lucas himself would take the remaining route, ensuring that each member of the team had a clear path to safety. "We'll rendezvous at the final safe house in 48 hours," he said. "Stay sharp and stay safe."

The Final Journey

AS THEY PREPARED TO leave the secondary safe house, the team took a moment to reflect on their journey. They had faced betrayal, survived deadly confrontations, and pulled off the heist of a lifetime. Now, they were in the final stretch of their escape.

"We've got this," Lucas said, his voice filled with determination. "Let's make it count."

Emma's Journey North

EMMA HEADED NORTH, using her tech skills to monitor the situation and stay one step ahead of any pursuit. She hacked into traffic cameras and police scanners, ensuring that she had real-time updates on their movements.

Her journey was tense, but her skills and determination carried her through. She used her knowledge of the area to find hidden routes and avoid detection, her mind focused on the task at hand.

Jack's Journey West

JACK HEADED WEST, USING his connections and smooth-talking skills to secure safe passage. He contacted old allies and arranged for temporary hideouts, ensuring that he had a clear path to safety.

His journey was filled with close calls and narrow escapes, but his confidence and resourcefulness carried him through. He used his charm and quick thinking to navigate the challenges, always staying one step ahead of the authorities.

Carl's Journey South

CARL HEADED SOUTH, using his strength and determination to handle any obstacles. He navigated the rough terrain and used his knowledge of the area to find hidden paths and secure hideouts.

His journey was physically demanding, but his resilience and determination carried him through. He used his strength and quick thinking to overcome the challenges, always staying focused on the task at hand.

Lucas's Journey East

LUCAS HEADED EAST, ensuring that each member of the team had a clear path to safety. He navigated the terrain with precision, using his knowledge of the area and his tactical skills to avoid detection.

His journey was filled with tense moments and close calls, but his determination and leadership carried him through. He used his skills and quick thinking to navigate the challenges, always staying focused on the task at hand.

The Final Rendezvous

AFTER 48 HOURS OF INTENSE travel and narrow escapes, the team finally reached the final safe house. The secluded cabin provided the perfect hideout, a place where they could regroup and plan their next move.

As they arrived one by one, the sense of relief and triumph was palpable. They had faced countless challenges and overcome them all, and now they were safe.

"We did it," Lucas said, his voice filled with pride. "We pulled off the impossible."

Emma, Jack, and Carl nodded, their faces reflecting a mixture of relief and triumph. They had made history, and they had done it together.

Reflections and New Beginnings

AS THEY SETTLED INTO the safe house, the team took a moment to reflect on their journey. They had faced betrayal, survived deadly confrontations, and completed the heist of a lifetime. Now, they were ready for whatever challenges and adventures the future might bring.

"We've proven that we're capable of anything," Lucas said, his voice filled with determination. "Whatever comes next, we'll face it together."

Emma, Jack, and Carl nodded, their confidence unwavering. They knew that their bond was unbreakable and that they were ready for whatever challenges lay ahead.

To the Future

AS THEY CELEBRATED their success, Lucas couldn't help but feel a sense of anticipation for the future. They had made history, and they were ready for whatever came next.

"To the future," Lucas said, raising a glass. "And to us."

The team clinked their glasses, their faces reflecting a mixture of relief and triumph. They had made history, and they had done it together.

As they looked to the future, they knew that they were ready for whatever challenges and adventures lay ahead. They had proven their resilience and their loyalty to each other, and they were ready to face whatever came next.

They had made history, and they were ready for whatever came next.

Chapter 14: The Aftermath

The early morning sun cast a warm glow over the secluded cabin that served as the team's final safe house. Lucas "Lucky" Kane stood outside, taking a moment to breathe in the fresh air and reflect on the journey that had brought them to this point. The heist had been a success, but the stakes were higher than ever. They had escaped law enforcement and reached their safe haven, but now came the real challenge: ensuring that their hard-earned spoils were divided fairly and navigating the delicate team dynamics.

Regrouping at the Safe House

INSIDE THE CABIN, THE atmosphere was tense but triumphant. Emma Hayes, the tech genius, was busy setting up her equipment to ensure their communications remained secure. Jack "Smooth" Taylor, the con artist, sat at the table, flipping a gold coin between his fingers with a thoughtful expression. Carl "Tank" Johnson, the muscle, was checking the perimeter, making sure they were not followed.

Lucas entered the cabin, his mind focused on the task ahead. "Alright, everyone," he began, drawing their attention. "We did it. We pulled off the heist of a lifetime. Now, it's time to count our spoils and plan our next steps."

Emma looked up from her laptop, her eyes sharp. "I've secured our comms and set up a monitoring system. We'll know if anyone tries to track us."

Jack leaned back in his chair, a grin spreading across his face. "So, how much did we actually get?"

Carl entered the room, closing the door behind him. "Perimeter's secure. Let's see what we've got."

The team gathered around the table, where several cases of gold and cash were laid out. Lucas opened the first case, revealing the glittering contents.

"We've got more than we could have imagined," he said, his voice filled with awe. "This is enough to set us all up for life."

Counting the Spoils

THE TEAM SPENT THE next hour counting and cataloging the spoils. The gold bars, cash, and other valuables were divided into equal shares, each member receiving a substantial amount.

Emma worked efficiently, using her tech skills to ensure that everything was accounted for. "We've got the totals," she said, her fingers flying over the keyboard. "Each of us will get an equal share. It's more than we ever dreamed of."

Jack's grin widened as he glanced at his share. "Looks like we hit the jackpot."

Carl's expression remained serious, though there was a glimmer of satisfaction in his eyes. "We earned every bit of this. But now comes the hard part—staying off the radar and enjoying it."

Tensions and Suspicions

AS THE TEAM REVELED in their success, a subtle shift in the atmosphere began to emerge. The realization of their newfound wealth brought with it the shadows of greed and suspicion. The high of the heist was wearing off, and the reality of their situation was setting in.

Emma, ever the pragmatist, voiced the concern that was on everyone's mind. "We need to talk about trust. We've come a long way together, but now we have to go our separate ways. How do we know that no one will double-cross the rest of us?"

Jack's grin faded, replaced by a thoughtful expression. "Emma's right. We need to be sure that everyone's on the level. No one wants to look over their shoulder for the rest of their life."

Carl crossed his arms, his face hardening. "Are you suggesting that one of us might try to take more than their share?"

The tension in the room was palpable. Lucas knew he had to address it before it escalated. "We've trusted each other through this entire process," he said, his voice calm but firm. "We've faced dangers together and come out on top. But I understand the concerns. Let's talk it out."

Navigating Team Dynamics

LUCAS'S LEADERSHIP skills were put to the test as he navigated the fractured team dynamics. He had to ensure that everyone felt heard and that their concerns were addressed. The success of the heist had brought them closer together, but the prospect of splitting up and going their separate ways was bringing old fears and insecurities to the surface.

"Emma, you've been our tech expert," Lucas began. "Your skills have been invaluable. What do you need to feel secure moving forward?"

Emma's gaze was steady. "I need assurances that no one will try to track or hack into our systems. We need to go completely dark."

Lucas nodded. "Agreed. We'll all go off the grid. New identities, new lives. No contact unless absolutely necessary."

Jack spoke up next. "I've got connections that can help us disappear. But I need to know that everyone's in agreement. No loose ends."

Carl's expression softened slightly. "I don't want any trouble either. We've earned this, and I want to enjoy it. But we need a pact—no one goes after another's share."

Lucas looked around the room, seeing the determination and resolve in each of their faces. "Alright, let's make it official. We each swear to respect each other's new lives and not interfere. We've come too far to let greed tear us apart."

The Pact

THE TEAM GATHERED AROUND the table, placing their hands on the pile of gold and cash. "We swear," Lucas said, his voice steady. "To respect each other's new lives, to never interfere, and to always remember the trust that brought us here."

Emma, Jack, and Carl repeated the oath, their voices filled with conviction. The pact was made, a solemn promise that bound them together even as they prepared to go their separate ways.

With the tension eased and the pact in place, the team began the final preparations for their new lives. Each member had a specific role to play, and they worked together to ensure that everything was in order.

Final Preparations

EMMA FOCUSED ON SECURING their digital footprints, ensuring that their new identities were untraceable. She set up encrypted communication channels and wiped all traces of their old lives from the internet.

Jack used his connections to arrange for new documents, passports, and bank accounts. He ensured that each member had the resources they needed to start fresh.

Carl handled the logistics, arranging for safe houses, transportation, and other essentials. His meticulous planning ensured that every detail was covered.

Lucas oversaw the entire process, coordinating their efforts and ensuring that nothing was overlooked. He knew that their survival depended on their ability to disappear completely.

Going Their Separate Ways

AS THE FINAL PREPARATIONS were completed, the team gathered for one last meeting. The atmosphere was somber but resolute. They had achieved their goal, but now it was time to say goodbye.

"We've come a long way together," Lucas said, his voice filled with emotion. "We've faced challenges and overcome them all. Now, it's time to go our separate ways. But remember, we're always connected by the trust and friendship we've built."

Emma, Jack, and Carl nodded, their faces reflecting a mixture of sadness and determination. They knew that this was the end of one chapter and the beginning of another.

Lucas handed each member their share of the spoils, along with their new documents and instructions for their new lives. "Take care of yourselves," he said, his voice steady. "And if you ever need anything, you know how to reach me."

One by one, the team members said their goodbyes. Emma hugged Lucas, her eyes filled with gratitude. "Thank you for everything, Lucas. I couldn't have done this without you."

Jack shook Lucas's hand, his grin returning. "It's been one hell of a ride. Take care, Lucky."

Carl's handshake was firm and sincere. "We did it, boss. Now, let's enjoy what we've earned."

As the team members left the cabin, Lucas watched them go, a sense of pride and satisfaction filling his heart. They had achieved the impossible and were now ready to face their new lives.

Reflections and New Beginnings

AS LUCAS STOOD ALONE in the cabin, he took a moment to reflect on their journey. They had faced betrayal, survived deadly confrontations, and completed the heist of a lifetime. Now, they were ready for whatever challenges and adventures the future might bring.

He knew that the bonds they had forged would never be broken, even as they went their separate ways. The trust and friendship that had brought them together would always be a part of their lives.

The New Path

WITH A DEEP BREATH, Lucas gathered his own share of the spoils and prepared to leave the cabin. He had a new life waiting for him, a fresh start filled with possibilities.

As he walked away from the cabin, Lucas felt a sense of freedom and anticipation. The journey had been long and arduous, but it had been worth it. They had made history, and now they were ready for whatever came next.

Lucas took one last look at the cabin, a smile playing on his lips. "To the future," he whispered, his voice filled with determination.

With that, he turned and walked into the dawn of a new day, ready to embrace the challenges and adventures that lay ahead.

Epilogue: The Legacy

YEARS LATER, THE LEGEND of the Fort Knox heist would still be spoken of in hushed tones. The masterminds behind the operation had disappeared without a trace, their identities and whereabouts a mystery. But for those who had been a part of it, the heist was more than just a job—it was a testament to their skills, determination, and the unbreakable bonds of trust they had forged.

Lucas, Emma, Jack, and Carl had gone their separate ways, each building a new life with the wealth they had earned. They had respected the pact they made, living in anonymity and enjoying the fruits of their labor.

But the memories of their journey together remained, a constant reminder of what they had achieved. And in quiet moments, they would think of each other, knowing that no matter where life took them, they would always be connected by the trust and friendship that had made them legends.

The Final Toast

IN A QUIET CORNER OF the world, Lucas raised a glass to the past and the future. "To us," he said, his voice filled with pride and gratitude. "And to the adventure that never ends."

As he drank to their legacy, he knew that their story was far from over. The bonds they had forged and the trust they had built would carry them through whatever came next. They had made history, and they were ready for whatever challenges and adventures the future might bring.

The legend of the Fort Knox heist would live on, a testament to their skills, determination, and the unbreakable bonds of trust that had made them legends. And as they looked to the future, they knew that they were ready for whatever came next.

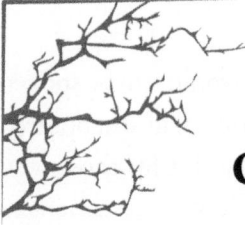

Chapter 15: The Twist

The team's journey from planning to execution of the Fort Knox heist had been a rollercoaster of tension, triumph, and betrayal. Each member of the team thought they knew the full story, but as they settled into their new lives, a shocking revelation was about to upend everything they believed about the heist and each other.

The True Mastermind Revealed

LUCAS "LUCKY" KANE sat in a small, nondescript cafe in an unfamiliar town. His new identity had afforded him a quiet life, far from the chaos of the heist. But a single message had drawn him back into the fray: "We need to meet. Urgent. – E."

Emma Hayes, the tech genius, had always been meticulous. If she said it was urgent, Lucas knew it was serious. As he waited for her arrival, he reflected on their journey. The heist had been his brainchild, but the smooth execution had been a team effort. Or so he thought.

Emma walked in, her eyes scanning the room before settling on Lucas. She slid into the seat opposite him, her expression grave. "Lucas, we've got a problem."

Lucas leaned forward, his attention fully on her. "What is it, Emma?"

She took a deep breath and handed him a dossier. "I've been digging into some files, trying to ensure our tracks are covered. But I found something—something that doesn't add up."

Lucas opened the dossier, his eyes widening as he read the contents. It detailed communications, transactions, and movements that pointed to a hidden player behind their heist. "This can't be right," he murmured. "There's no way."

Emma nodded. "I thought the same, but it's all there. The real mastermind behind our heist wasn't us, Lucas. It was someone pulling the strings from the shadows."

Hidden Motives and Secret Alliances

AS LUCAS AND EMMA DELVED deeper into the dossier, a clearer picture began to emerge. It seemed that their heist had been orchestrated by a figure known only as "The Broker." This mysterious individual had manipulated events and people, ensuring that Lucas's team would carry out the heist while remaining oblivious to the larger scheme.

"I've been tracing The Broker's activities," Emma explained. "They've been involved in numerous high-profile heists and criminal activities, always staying behind the scenes. And they had a mole in our team."

Lucas's heart sank. "A mole? Who?"

Emma's face was grim. "It's Jack. He's been feeding information to The Broker from the start. Every move we made, every plan we discussed—Jack was relaying it all."

The realization hit Lucas like a punch to the gut. Jack, the smooth-talking con artist he had trusted implicitly, had betrayed them. "Why? What's in it for him?"

Emma shrugged. "Power, money, protection—who knows? But we need to act fast. The Broker's network is vast, and they'll come for us once they realize we know the truth."

Facing Their Fates

LUCAS AND EMMA KNEW they needed to regroup and confront Jack. They reached out to Carl "Tank" Johnson, who was living under a new identity in a remote part of the country. The reunion was tense, with emotions running high.

Carl listened to their explanation, his face growing darker with each revelation. "Jack betrayed us? I trusted that son of a bitch."

"We all did," Lucas said, his voice heavy with betrayal. "But we need to confront him and figure out how to deal with The Broker. This isn't over yet."

They tracked Jack to a luxurious villa in an undisclosed location. As they approached, the opulence of his new life stood in stark contrast to their more modest accommodations. It was clear that Jack had profited significantly from his dealings with The Broker.

Jack greeted them with his characteristic charm, but there was an edge to his demeanor. "Lucas, Emma, Carl—what brings you to my humble abode?"

Lucas didn't waste any time. "Cut the crap, Jack. We know you've been working with The Broker. You've been feeding them information about us and the heist."

Jack's smile faltered, replaced by a cold, calculating look. "I see you've been busy. Yes, I've been in contact with The Broker. But it's not what you think."

Emma stepped forward, her anger barely contained. "Then tell us what it is, Jack. Why betray us?"

Jack sighed, his facade of confidence slipping. "It's complicated. The Broker approached me before the heist. They offered me protection and a substantial payout if I helped facilitate the heist from the inside. I didn't have a choice."

Carl's fists clenched at his sides. "There's always a choice, Jack. You chose to betray us."

Before the confrontation could escalate, the sound of approaching vehicles filled the air. Lucas's instincts kicked in. "We need to move. Now."

The Law Closes In

AS THEY RUSHED TO LEAVE, law enforcement vehicles surrounded the villa. It was clear that The Broker had tipped off the authorities, intending to clean up loose ends.

"We're trapped," Emma said, her voice filled with panic. "What do we do, Lucas?"

Lucas's mind raced, searching for a way out. "We split up. It's our best chance. Emma, you take the back exit and head to the safe house we discussed. Carl, you and Jack find another way out. I'll create a diversion."

The team scattered, each member moving with the urgency and precision that had carried them through the heist. Lucas sprinted to the front of the villa, drawing the attention of the law enforcement officers.

"Over here!" he shouted, firing a few shots into the air. The officers converged on his location, allowing Emma, Carl, and Jack to make their escape.

The Final Move

AS LUCAS EVADED THE officers, he knew that the real fight was just beginning. The Broker's influence was far-reaching, and they would stop at nothing to eliminate any threats to their operation. Lucas needed to find a way to turn the tables and expose The Broker's network.

Reaching the safe house, Lucas found Emma and Carl waiting, their faces filled with concern. "What now, Lucas?" Emma asked. "We can't keep running forever."

Lucas's mind was already working on a plan. "We need to go public. Expose The Broker's network and their involvement in the heist. It's risky, but it's our best shot."

Carl nodded. "I'll back you up, whatever it takes."

Emma was already working on her laptop, her fingers flying over the keys. "I'm hacking into The Broker's communication channels. If we can find something concrete, we can take it to the authorities and the media."

As they worked together, the tension in the room was palpable. They knew that failure was not an option. The Broker's network was powerful, but they had one advantage: the element of surprise.

The Revelation

EMMA'S SKILLS PAID off as she unearthed a trove of incriminating evidence. Communications, transaction records, and surveillance footage that linked The Broker to the heist and numerous other criminal activities.

"This is it," Emma said, her voice filled with excitement. "We've got them."

Lucas nodded. "Good work, Emma. Now we need to get this to the authorities and the media. We'll need to go public and expose The Broker's entire operation."

As they prepared to release the information, Jack entered the safe house, his face pale and his demeanor subdued. "I'm sorry," he said, his voice filled with regret. "I never wanted it to come to this."

Lucas looked at him, his expression unreadable. "It's not too late, Jack. Help us take down The Broker. Redeem yourself."

Jack nodded, a look of determination in his eyes. "I'll do whatever it takes."

The Final Showdown

WITH JACK'S HELP, THE team coordinated a plan to release the evidence to the media and the authorities simultaneously. They knew that The Broker would retaliate, but they were prepared to face whatever came next.

The media frenzy that followed was unprecedented. The exposure of The Broker's network sent shockwaves through the criminal underworld and law enforcement agencies alike. Arrests were made, and The Broker's influence began to crumble.

But The Broker was not one to go down without a fight. As the team monitored the situation, they received a chilling message: "You've made a grave mistake. This isn't over."

The final showdown came swiftly. The Broker's enforcers tracked the team to their safe house, leading to a tense and deadly confrontation. Bullets flew, and the sound of gunfire echoed through the night.

Lucas, Emma, Jack, and Carl fought with everything they had, their determination and unity carrying them through. In the end, they emerged victorious, but not without cost. Carl was injured, and the safe house was compromised.

The Lasting Impact

WITH THE BROKER'S NETWORK dismantled and their immediate threat eliminated, the team faced the reality of their situation. They had survived, but the journey had taken its toll.

Lucas knew that their lives would never be the same. The heist had changed them, forging bonds that would last a lifetime. But it had also exposed them to dangers and betrayals that left scars.

As they prepared to go their separate ways once more, Lucas gathered the team for one final meeting. "We did it," he said, his voice filled with pride and determination. "We took down The Broker and exposed their network. We've made a lasting impact."

Emma, Jack, and Carl nodded, their faces reflecting a mixture of relief and determination. They knew that their journey was far from over, but they were ready to face whatever came next.

A New Beginning

AS THEY PARTED WAYS, Lucas felt a sense of closure and anticipation. The heist had been just the beginning, a catalyst for change that would shape their futures. They had faced challenges, betrayals, and dangers, but they had emerged stronger and more united.

Lucas took one last look at the safe house, a smile playing on his lips. "To the future," he whispered, his voice filled with determination.

With that, he turned and walked into the dawn of a new day, ready to embrace the challenges and adventures that lay ahead. The legend of the Fort Knox heist would live on, a testament to their skills, determination, and the unbreakable bonds of trust that had made them legends.

And as they looked to the future, they knew that they were ready for whatever challenges and adventures the future might bring. They had made history, and they were ready for whatever came next.

Don't miss out!

Visit the website below and you can sign up to receive emails whenever William James Brown publishes a new book. There's no charge and no obligation.

https://books2read.com/r/B-A-MCMXB-ZQXIF

BOOKS 2 READ

Connecting independent readers to independent writers.

About the Author

William James Brown is a versatile author known for gripping thriller fiction, from espionage and psychological suspense to legal dramas and supernatural mysteries. His compelling narratives and unpredictable twists keep readers enthralled in the depths of human intrigue and suspenseful plots.

Milton Keynes UK
Ingram Content Group UK Ltd.
UKHW030142051224
452010UK00001B/204

9 798227 275295